DEATH BY ANALYSIS

DEATH BY ANALYSIS
Another Adventure from Inspector Canal's New York Agency

Bruce Fink

Any resemblance between Inspector Canal and actual persons,
living or dead, might well be intentional.
All other characters are substantially fictional.

KARNAC

First published in 2013 by
Karnac Books Ltd
118 Finchley Road
London NW3 5HT

British Library Cataloguing in Publication Data

A C.I.P. for this book is available from the British Library

ISBN-13: 978-1-78220-031-4

Typeset by V Publishing Solutions Pvt Ltd., Chennai, India

Printed in Great Britain

www.karnacbooks.com

That death's unnatural that kills for loving.

—Shakespeare

Symptoms speak even to those who do not know how to hear them. Nor do they tell the whole story even to those who do.

—A certain French psychoanalyst

Returning home after an invigorating run in Central Park, and seating himself in front of the piano where he had been looking forward to playing around with a melody that had been going through his head that morning as he loped along the wooded paths, Inspector Canal noticed that a message had been left for him in the usual location just to the right of the keyboard. Deliberately ignoring it for some minutes as he translated into finger motions the air that had come to him through no bidding of his own, the purportedly retired French Secret Serviceman, who had moved to New York some years earlier, eventually stopped and glanced over at the note on the salver. Inspector Ponlevek of the New York Police Department had called to say he would stop by at around four to discuss a recent death at a psychoanalytic institute and hoped Canal was willing and had no prior engagements. Wondering what it could possibly have to do with him, or with Ponlevek for that matter, that yet another aged analyst had died in the saddle—of boredom, no doubt—Canal's fingers continued to dance over the ivories for some time before heeding the call of the hot shower.

CHAPTER ONE

Greeting with a warm handshake the square-jawed NYPD inspector with whom he had worked once before, Canal invited Ponlevek into his cozy study. Offering him a seat and the regulation Coca-Cola, even though it ran roughshod over the tea called for by the afternoon hour, Canal commented, "It has been quite some time, *mon cher* Ponlevek," pronouncing the American's name with a French accent, as he did virtually every other English word, prone as he was to enunciate every *th* like z and every *is* like *ease*, not to mention his patent proclivity to drop his *h's*. "What 'as it been, about a year and a 'alf?"

The towering man in blue—whose prior acquaintance with Canal had forced him to overcome his initial annoyance at having his name pronounced as if he descended from a long line of French cheeses—nodded, seated himself in a comfortable armchair, and accepted the glass that his elder held out to him.

"How is the liquidity crisis coming along?" Canal asked, flashing the American a broad smile.

Ponlevek balked momentarily. Having been in analysis for the past eighteen months, he had finally begun to be attuned to double entendres and he now recalled that the former Secret Serviceman was especially fond of them. What he did not remember was whether Canal had gotten wind of his occasional bouts of erectile dysfunction, or of "Mr. Ed" as he preferred to call it, during their work on the case of the liquidity squeeze. His fiancée, special agent Erica Simmons of the FBI, had become rather chummy with the Frenchman during that case—far too chummy for Ponlevek's liking—and it struck him as not impossible that she had dropped hints about it to the *frog*, that being the consecrated term of unendearment with which he liked to think of Canal owing to the somewhat underhanded trick the older man had played on him. The inspector might, however, simply be referring to New York City's financial crisis, so Ponlevek decided upon a reply that would commit him to neither construction. "Much improved," he said, affecting nonchalance.

Canal noticed the noncommittal repartee. "The newspapers I have read seem to suggest as much, at any rate," he proffered, as if to say that the banking fiasco were precisely what he had meant by "liquidity crisis," while he poured himself a cup of tea. "Although it is hard to know whether to believe them or simply view them as trying to convey the impression that there is no cause for alarm."

"Da jury's still out on dat one, I tink it's safe to say," the New Yorker commented with his thickish Queens accent.

"Let us drink zen," Canal exclaimed, lifting his cup, "to liquidity—may it flow in ever better health!"

They each tasted their respective beverages, and as Canal seated himself on the couch, Ponlevek seized the floor before Canal could slip another mine under it for him to tread on. "I was hoping you would be willing to help me with a rather confusing case."

The Frenchman looked over at the American and gave his head a slight tilt upward, as if to say, "Go on."

"There's been a murder at an analytic institute in Manhattan—"

"A murder? You mean it was not just someone dying of boredom?"

The surprised expression on Ponlevek's face led Canal to go on, "Psychoanalysts have been known to die of boredom, you know. I would not be surprised if it had happened to some of their patients too. Many analysts these days consider it taboo to ever ask a question or encourage a patient to talk about anything that he has not brought up himself, so they almost never say anything or ask about anything. They believe it is part of their own so-called countertransference to—"

"Really?" Ponlevek cried. "It's hard to picture. In my own experience ..." The detective stopped himself in mid-sentence, trying to recall whether Canal did or did not know he was in analysis. Then, deciding that the Frenchman might lay off on the innuendo if he knew, he continued, "With Jack Lovett, it's nothing like that. I can't imagine either of us ever dying of boredom." Reflecting for a moment, he added, "Well, maybe *him*."

Canal could well imagine how his friend Jack, whose number he had given to Ponlevek's fiancée, recommending she try to convince her beau to go see him, might grow bored listening to the police officer. But he turned to the supposed reason for Ponlevek's visit. "So when and where did this murder take place?"

"The weekend before last at the Forbes Convention Center, where a big meeting was being held by the New Institute for Psychoanalytic Psychoanalysis on the Lower East Side."

"You are not serious, are you? It's really called the Institute for Psychoanalytic Psychoanalysis?"

"That's what it says on all their brochures."

"As if there could be *un*psychoanalytic psychoanalysis ..." Then, stretching backward for a moment, Canal added, "Well I guess there is quite a lot of that going around these days."

"As you can imagine, I'm a bit out of my depth here."

5

Canal could imagine, but was thinking about something else. "Let me get this straight, the acronym for this institute is N-I-P-P, and then L-E-S for Lower East Side."

"Right. They all call it NIPLESS, or NIP for short."

"But what it actually spells is NIPPLES!"

"I guess so," the New Yorker acquiesced. Then, chuckling, he added, "I never thought of it that way."

"At least somebody down there must have a sense of humor," Canal quipped. "How long has this institute been around? I do not believe I have ever heard of it before. Then again, there must be something like forty such institutes in New York City alone."

"From what I've been able to gather," responded Ponlevek, "it was founded in the early nineteen-eighties. A small group of analysts left one of those uptown institutes because they thought it was too snooty, run like a British club. But based on what I've heard, it's hard to say if it's really any more liberal or informal than the club—I mean, institute—they left. The main difference mentioned to me by one of the trainees was that they call each other by their first names instead of their last like they do uptown."

Canal smiled at this, well aware that breakaway groups often reproduced exactly the same hierarchical structures that supposedly bothered them so much in the organization they broke away from, confining their revolution to taking the place of the people at the top. "So one of the old training analysts," the inspector surmised, "who wielded a little too much—"

"Training what?" Ponlevek broke in.

Canal's bushy eyebrows raised of their own accord, but his surprise soon abated. "Of course, it is only natural that, as an ordinary analysand, you would not know about such absurdities—"

"Ordinary what?" asked the New Yorker who was feeling increasingly at sea.

6

"Analysand, a person who analyzes himself, or herself as the case may be."

"Isn't that what the shrink is supposed to do?" asked Ponlevek, believing he was merely stating the obvious.

"Not if he has anything under the coffeemaker." Noticing Ponlevek's blank stare, Canal explained the colloquial French formulation that had just popped into his mind, "Not if he has any sense in his head. Have you not noticed that Jack Lovett mostly just helps you analyze yourself?"

The man in blue reflected. "I guess so, now that you mention it. Seems like quite a racket."

"Yes, I suppose it might seem somewhat paradoxical at first to pay someone else to make you work, but people do much the same thing when they hire personal trainers or music teachers." Canal sipped his tea thoughtfully. "In any case, the chattier the analyst, the more likely the therapy is to amount to mere suggestion or counseling."

As Canal seemed to have become distracted by some thought or other, and was looking down into his cup, Ponlevek prodded him. "You were saying something about some old analyst who was out of training wielding something or other?"

"Not exactly," Canal replied, looking up. "I was conjecturing that one of the old training analysts—"

"You mean there are old analysts who are still in training?"

"Would that there were," the Frenchman exclaimed warmly. "No, in most American institutes, there are certain big shots who grant themselves the exclusive right to analyze the students admitted to the program who wish to become psychoanalysts themselves. The big shots consider themselves to be the only ones capable of conducting training analyses—"

"What are those?" Ponlevek queried before Canal could go any further into this uncharted territory.

"Analyses that allow patients to become analysts themselves."

"What difference is there between a training analysis and any other analysis?"

"None, as far as I can tell. Either you do an analysis or you don't. Why one analysis should be considered to make you capable of conducting analyses yourself and another not is beyond me." He contemplated his teacup again. "Officially speaking, though, a training analysis is an analysis you do with a training analyst, whether it is any good or not. So it is all quite tautological."

Canal looked up from his teacup and went on, "In any case, the band of training analysts at an institute usually makes it very difficult for anyone else to become a training analyst, and in that way they endeavor to ensure that every new student goes through what they think is the right kind of analysis and at the same time assure themselves plenty of patients—well at least one or two *real* analysands, given how few of them actually do analysis anymore, seeing most of their patients only once a week."

"So these training analysts are the ones at the top of the totem pole?" Ponlevek cut to what he considered to be the chase.

Canal nodded. "They have a tendency to brandish a ridiculous amount of power within their institutes—"

"Must make them a lot of friends," the inspector quipped, thinking of Olivetti, his direct superior down at headquarters.

"Yes, which is why I postulated that one of them, despite being called by his first name, must have been murdered by one of NIPPLES's discontents."

"Well, I'm sorry to say," Ponlevek began, even though he was by no means sorry, "it wasn't one of the old training analysts whose number came up, not by a long shot." He savored this rare moment of being able to contradict one of the Frenchman's almost invariably accurate suppositions. "In fact it was one of the youngest students who got whacked, in a manner of speaking, that is."

"You mean the student was not exactly whacked?"

"No. She was murdered in a far more subtle way, with poison."

Canal listened attentively, merely raising an eyebrow.

"The coroner found a small prick mark on her arm and traces of curare in her bloodstream," the detective added, examining Canal's features closely to see if he would recognize the poison in question.

"Quite creative, using the derivative of a little-known plant that few autopsists would ever think of testing for. I'm surprised the boys downtown bothered to look for it."

"Well," responded Ponlevek, despite his disappointment that Canal did seem to know something about curare, "when a twenty-nine-year-old girl with no known medical condition, and who is about to receive the student-of-the-year award, drops dead at a conference dinner with three hundred guests, they make a special effort down at the morgue. The lab tells me this poison was used centuries ago by South American Indian tribes to paralyze animals they were hunting. Comes from a plant almost completely unknown in North America—they called it something like *Rhododendron tormentos*."

"*Chondrodendron tomentosum*," Canal corrected him off-handedly. "It was occasionally used here a long time ago to induce temporary paralysis for medical purposes, since it has a peculiar effect on the body: it relaxes and then paralyzes the patient's skeletal muscles while the heart goes on beating." Sipping his tea, he added, "So you have to figure out who could have gotten a hold of such a rare plant—actually there are a few possible ones, including *Strychnos toxifera*."

Ponlevek breathed in as though he were about to speak, but the Frenchman, whose mind had shifted into overdrive, did not hear and added, "It might actually be easier to see if any of the suspects use words containing the root 'cure' in their speech, like curative, curate, curious, curator, curiosity, Q-Tip—"

"Q-Tip?" Ponlevek exclaimed. "Sounds like pretty slippery stuff to base an accusation of murder on!"

"Perhaps I *was* exaggerating with Q-Tip ... I obviously did not mean to suggest that would suffice to justify an accusation—merely a suspicion. You might also want to keep an ear out for unusual related words, such as chronometer, rhododendron, tomatoes, tormentor, memento, and the like."

"I can't see what possible bearing chronology and pimento could have on the case," Ponlevek protested, confused.

"Chronometer and memento. You need to pay attention to the words people employ if you are to attend to the insistence of the letter in ze signifying chain."

"In ze what?" Ponlevek asked, inadvertently imitating the other's accent. "In *the* what?" he rectified his pronunciation, trying to enunciate the digraph without a Queens accent for a change.

"Let me try to explain it to you simply."

Ponlevek nodded appreciatively.

"Let us imagine there was something you wanted to hide from your fiancée, Erica—say the fact that you had been flirting with a cute blond down at the police station."

"I'd never do anything of the kind," Ponlevek declared obstreperously.

"I am not saying you would, I am simply asking you to imagine it for a moment." As Ponlevek finally nodded assent to the hypothetical, Canal went on, "Let us suppose her name is Doris." The Frenchman noted with satisfaction that the NYPD inspector gulped at this, convincing the former that he had correctly recalled the name of the switchboard operator he had spoken with once or twice down at the police station. "What is likely to happen when you are with Erica?"

Ponlevek pondered for a moment, but as his thoughts instantaneously turned to Mr. Ed, he quickly feigned ignorance, "I don't know."

"Since Doris has been on your mind and you are trying to hide that fact from Erica—you are perhaps even trying especially hard not to think about Doris while you are

10

with Erica—you are likely to introduce words into your conversations with Erica that you might not ordinarily use, words that are somehow related to Doris—like porous or dork, or you might find yourself suddenly talking about Dorian or Boris. Since Doris is blond, you might find words like fond, bond, blind, or even yellow cropping up in your speech when you least expect it."

"Really?" Ponlevek asked, astonished. "I've never noticed anything like that before."

"Well, start paying attention and I suspect you will. When someone is trying to hide something, and yet simultaneously can't help but throw it in another person's face or confess to it and receive punishment from that person, there are lots of tell-tale signs that slip out, if only one knows how to read them."

"Well, I've questioned quite a few people down at the Institute and can't recall anyone mentioning anything like curative or chronometer, but I'll keep it in mind."

"You might try detecting this sort of thing in yourself first," Canal recommended. "It might be topics you chatted about with Doris that insistently come to mind when you are with Erica, or some weather report or news item she told you about. You will recognize the topics as soon as you hear yourself talk about them, and eventually recognize them even before you begin talking about them. You generally know better than anyone else what you are trying to hide, and so can easily become aware of things related to it that slip out."

"I guess so," Ponlevek submitted, although he would have wagered good money that Canal knew better than he did what the New Yorker might be trying to hide. "The fact is," the NYPD inspector added, and it was clear from the expression on his face that he was pleased as punch with himself regarding what was to follow, "I have already figured out who had access to curare."

Canal's eyebrows rose to half-mast. "What do you need my help for, then, if you already know who did the deed?"

11

"I'm not having trouble with the who but with the how," Ponlevek explained.

Canal eyed his interlocutor narrowly. "But when you do not know the how," he opined, "you cannot be sure of the who—there could be more than one."

"Exactly," Ponlevek concurred, impressed once again that the Frenchman had divined the conundrum.

"Tell me about this girl who was murdered. What do you know about her?"

Content to move onto less slippery ground, Ponlevek became more expansive. "Doreen's something of a mystery, as far as I can tell. Everyone I spoke with said she was as sweet as could be and had nothing but the highest praise for her—some even called her a tremendous asset to the program. They thought her the last person to have enemies and couldn't imagine why anyone would want to hurt her, much less kill her."

"*Manque d'imagination*," Canal proclaimed. Perceiving Ponlevek's uncomprehending features, he added, "They could not imagine, and yet they of all people should have been able to."

"They all commented on what an attractive blond she was, and judging from the pictures of her I saw, I'd have to agree. No surviving family. An older brother died in a car wreck over a decade ago and her parents passed away a bit more recently, leaving her a bundle," the New Yorker reported. "Apparently had everything—money, looks, style, a promising career, and a ton of well-wishers in her training program. A real shame," he concluded, shrugging his shoulders.

"What about this suspect of yours, the one with access to curare?"

"Not an easy bird to flush out," proffered Ponlevek, patently proud that he had managed to do so. "She's an anthropologist at City University. Specializes in Amazonian tribes."

Canal nodded, conscious of the relevance of her occupation to the lethal substance involved in the crime. "What is her connection to NIPPLES?"

"Married for thirty years to a faculty member there, but recently divorced, owing, she told me, to her husband's fascination with a student at the Institute. Claimed she didn't know which one." The American gave Canal a significant look.

"*Le crime passionnel,* uncontrolled jealousy?" the Frenchman wondered aloud, stroking his beardless chin. "What made you think to question her?"

"An offhanded remark," Ponlevek replied, hoping Canal might notice that the New Yorker had gleaned something from working with him, "made by one of the NIPPLES staff—I believe it was the librarian—about Doreen being very friendly with a senior analyst by the name of William Watkins."

"*Chercher* l'autre *femme,*" mused Canal half-aloud. "Good thinking," he added, smiling at Ponlevek. "What is the problem with the how?"

"The female Dr. Watkins, Wilma is her name, wasn't anywhere near the convention center where the crime was committed—has an alibi solid as a rock."

"As a rock? It cannot be rocked?"

"No dice—I tried everything imaginable."

"So you figure that …"

"She must've had an accomplice, someone on the inside, someone who attended the conference and administered the poison. I'm hoping that you can help me figure out who it was and how it was done."

"But an accomplice would have to have a motive of her or his own. Unless the accessory was unaware of the lethal nature of the substance and thought it was some sort of mickey …"

The New Yorker nodded meditatively at the manifold lines of thought this opened up.

"Tell me all about the circumstances of her death and the different people you have questioned so far," said the Frenchman, his curiosity piqued by the complexity of the case.

By the time Ponlevek had filled Canal in on the details of the young woman's death and his impressions of the various people at the Institute with whom he had thus far spoken, all of whom had struck him as pretty smooth characters, it was getting on for supper time. The retiree offered the detective a taste of his *ordinaire*, nothing special having been arranged in advance for a dinner guest, but Ponlevek bowed out, saying he had prior plans to meet Erica for dinner in Chinatown.

Canal promised to consider helping his friend out but, saying that he was not yet sure how to proceed, gave Ponlevek no specific time or date on which to meet at NIPPLES's offices. The latter was disappointed by this shilly-shallying, but had to content himself with Canal's pledge to give it some serious thought.

CHAPTER TWO

Sipping sherry that evening at the Scentury Club, Inspector Canal's home away from home in Manhattan, the elegantly attired Frenchman sank into a soft armchair at the same time as he sank into a deep reverie. It was getting well on for fall and the beautiful orange and red maples would soon be peaking, color-wise at least, in northern New England. Owing to one thing or another requiring his attention, the inspector had not yet found or forged an opportunity to hike or bike for a few days in northern Vermont and southern Quebec around Lake Memphremagog, that large, beautiful expanse of water, as the Native Americans put it, a.k.a. Lac Brome. Were he to take on this murder case with Ponlevek, who knew how long it would be before he could get away from New York?

Perhaps he could leave early tomorrow morning and be back in time to help out ... As odd and intriguing as it was, the girl was already dead, and the crime had been committed over a week ago—what difference would it make if the accomplice were found a week earlier or later?

Shifting in the armchair, it suddenly occurred to Canal that the murderer might have more than one target at the Institute ... the fascinated, straying husband, for instance. Ponlevek had not been able to hold the anthropologist on circumstantial evidence alone and could do no more than put her under surreptitious surveillance. Still, she and her accessory would be on their guard, given the presence of coppers like Ponlevek hanging around the NIPPLES clinic, and might be expected to wait until things cooled down a little.

Then again—a new train of thought drifted through his mind—if it were a crime of fury and the murderer's passions were still on the boil ... He comforted himself with the considerations that emotions rarely remained at the boiling point for more than a few hours at a time and that poison was hardly the most common instrument employed in crimes of passion. Still—

His internal monologue was interrupted at this point by a firm, repeated tapping on the shoulder. A man of similar carriage to Canal's had been patiently standing in front of him for a few moments, and had even called his name a couple of times. The man had eventually resigned himself to taking a seat in the armchair alongside Canal, ordering fresh drinks for both of them, and, once they had arrived, to physically intruding upon Canal's abstraction only when he had finally noticed a relaxing of his facial muscles.

"Well, aren't we lost in thought like a modern-day Socrates?" the new arrival exclaimed once Canal showed signs of life and recognition. "Fortunately you take the precaution of sitting down first, unlike the Silenus from Athens. We are not all blessed with his exquisite sense of balance."

"*Mon cher Jacques*," Canal cried warmly, eagerly shaking the hand of one of his closest friends in Manhattan, Jack Lovett, the well-known New York psychoanalyst. "What a pleasant surprise! I did not notice you here when I first arrived—have you been at the club long?"

"Just long enough to watch your face go through a dozen different contortions," the analyst with a rather unruly shock of red hair replied, smiling. He was wearing a dark brown sweater and his usual professorial corduroy jacket of an indiscernible

16

tannish hue, complete with slightly worn elbow patches, which was at least suitable for the autumnal season. "Although I am unable to divine silent cogitations like C. Auguste Dupin, I am sure you are up to no good." Lovett knew whereof he spoke, having had first-hand knowledge of a couple of Canal's escapades and indiscretions.

"Not yet," Canal bantered back jovially, and the two men laughed together and then lifted their glasses to future exploits. Ostensibly waxing serious, Canal asked his companion, "Tell me, what do you know about nipples?"

The American was only somewhat taken aback, having known Canal for several years already, and confined his response to the bipedal, "Come again?"

"Nipples," Canal reiterated. Then realizing the ambiguous nature of this enunciation, he added, "Or, if you prefer, nipless, that psychoanalytic institute on the Lower East Side."

Lovett's eyes brightened. "Quite the name they chose, isn't it," he quipped, smiling. Then, looking squarely at Canal, he said, "It just so happens that I know a great deal about the place—why do you ask?"

"I have been asked by the police to look into something that happened down there—"

"I think I can imagine by whom you were asked."

"I'm sure you can," Canal assented, winking at his interlocutor with whom Ponlevek was in analysis. "The problem is, I have never heard of the place before and don't know any of its history. What can you tell me about it?"

"Do you have all night? I was one of the site visitors sent to evaluate and report to the central committee of the American Psychoanalytic Establishment on—"

"Yes, APE," Canal interjected. "I've always liked that acronym."

"Why am I not surprised?" Lovett retorted, just the slightest bit miffed. "You know very well, of course, that they go by APsaE."

17

"Yes," Canal winked, "to distinguish themselves from the other eight-hundred pound gorillas in town, the American Psychological Establishment and the American Psychiatric Establishment."

"As I was saying, I was a member of the accreditation committee sent to investigate the conflicts there a couple of years ago and am rather intimately acquainted with the workings of NIPPLES."

"I am in luck, then," Canal jubilated. "Tell me all about the conflicts."

"With pleasure," replied the psychoanalyst, who always enjoyed spinning a good yarn, especially for an attentive listener like Canal, his *alter idem amicissimus*, as he thought of his friend. "But not here, Quesjac. You never know who might overhear and who might know whom or be in analysis with whom."

"Quite right," Canal concurred, looking around at the different people seated in the large salon.

"My place is but a few short steps from here. Why don't you come up and I'll offer you some *bernache* I received this morning from a couple of vintners I know out on the tip of Long Island?"

"People drink *bernache* on Long Island? *Première nouvelle!*" Canal exclaimed stentorianly.

"My vintner friends are French, naturally. Their brew is not half-bad and is a nice way to kick off the harvest season."

CHAPTER THREE

Lovett's finely appointed Madison Avenue apartment commanded an expansive view of the area between midtown and Central Park, and his red grape juice from the northern tip of Long Island, which had just barely begun to ferment and was only about three or four percent alcohol, made for a nice, albeit unusual, late night drink.

Canal, who had not been to his friend's apartment for some months, perceived that a new decorative item, Watteau's fabulously expensive *Les Bergers*, had been given pride of place in Lovett's living room. It supplanted the totally different Calder that had previously occupied the same spot on the wall to which the eye was naturally drawn due to the way the furniture was arranged. He wondered for a brief moment whether Lovett might possibly have felt compelled to acquire—presumably by legal means, unlike his own rather more dubious methods—a Watteau just because Canal happened to have had one hanging in his study for the past year and a half, although it would not grace his walls much longer, he reflected regretfully. Was Lovett as competitive with him as this seemed to suggest?

The inspector had first suspected his American pal of coveting whatever the Frenchman possessed when, a number of years back, he observed that Lovett bought himself a seven-foot Steinway after seeing the Bosendorfer in Canal's study, even though the analyst could not pick out the slightest little tune on the piano. The latter's supererogatory purchase had nevertheless been bested, Canal reflected not without a certain modicum of satisfaction and even a little *rire sous cape*, when the Frenchman had managed, through certain long-cultivated connections of his in Nantes, to acquire a similarly large Steinway built exclusively in Germany—it being well known in the finer musical circles that the beauty and depth of sound produced by the pianos built in Hamburg far surpassed that produced by the instruments built by the selfsame company in New York.

The Frenchman put the question of the American's possibly rivalrous feelings toward him aside for the time being and, once the two men were comfortably ensconced in the armchairs around the coffee table, repeated his question to Lovett regarding what he knew about NIPPLES.

"Most of these schools are, as you undoubtedly know," Lovett began professorially, "born out of discord within the schools that preceded them. This particular institute split off in the early nineteen-eighties from the main institute in New York affiliated with APE, the New Yorkers' Psychoanalytic Society—"

"Yes, the hard-drinking nips," Canal nodded, indicating that he was familiar with the NYPS. "Is that not the one you belong to?"

Lovett nodded, "It was at the time I participated in that site visit a couple of years ago. I've since left."

Canal's brow rose involuntarily.

"Left, yes, and my departure was due in no small part to the lack of action taken by APE to deal with the abuses rampant at NIPPLES." Lovett made no attempt now to spell out the name of the Lower East Side institute or pretend it should be pronounced "nipless." "I'm fed up with the whole institutional framework supposedly designed for the preservation and transmission of psychoanalysis," he declaimed with some heat. "I just work with a few friends now in a study group."

Canal was impressed, but uttered no sound to interrupt the analyst's revelations.

"NIPPLES was born out of one of the last splits for ideological reasons allowed by APE, the Calanians finally having managed to convince APE to let them break away from the Clanians after relentless struggles between the two factions. The aging Clanians had ruled NYPI, the training institute associated with NYPS, with an iron fist for several decades. But, in a complicated and protracted power play, the Calanians wrested control of the society from the Clanians."

Canal shook his head. "You are going too fast for me—who are these Calanians? I do not believe I have ever heard of them before."

"I never quite understood where the name came from," Lovett admitted. "For a while I thought it must have come from the area around the Calanques in the south of France between Marseilles and Cassis ..."

"I assume Clanian and Calanian are spelled in such a way that the only differance between them is the letter *a*?" the Frenchman surmised, pronouncing the final syllable of *difference* like *ants*.

"Pretty unbelievable, isn't it?!"

Canal whistled appreciatively. "I thought these trends were usually named after *une tête pensante*, some influential theorist like Winnicott or Kohut," he protested, perplexed.

"Not invariably," Lovett explained. "There have, after all, been the culturalists, subjectivists, objectivists, intersubjectivists, outer-objectivists, and relationalists, to mention just a few."

"Huh," Canal uttered a guttural sound. "Nevertheless, those schools all adopted names that captured or at least tried to characterize their theoretical orientations. With these Calanians, *il y a quelque chose que je ne m'explique pas*." Cognizant of Lovett's command of French, the Frenchman did not bother to paraphrase himself in English. Casting about for an explanation of the curious name, Canal enquired, "Were there any theoretical differences between the Clanians and the Calanians?"

"Oh yes, huge differences! The two different approaches had wholly different vocabularies, and even when they used the same technical terms, they assigned totally different meanings to them, making it such that people from the one school could barely understand people from the other. Meetings would break down into riotous affairs where half the auditorium would insist on conceptualizing childhood development as a random series of ruptures and the other half as a well-ordered series of stages, and the shouting would get louder and louder, each group hoping to silence the other by reiterating its mantra-like formulations ever more stridently." At this, the analyst laughed mirthlessly, recalling the nefarious effects such obvious warfare—presented under the guise of scientific debate—had had on the training of many of his own generation, himself included.

"So the *a* is perhaps privative, as in aporia," Canal mused aloud, "even though it appears within the name instead of before—"

The inspector's musings were interrupted by the sudden entrance into the living room of a shapely brunette in a skirt surprisingly short for one with her hair in a bun and horn-rimmed glasses adorning her face.

"Sorry to interrupt, Dr. Lovett, but I've just finished for the day," she said in a partly professional, partly alluring tone of voice. "I'm afraid there was a lot more to do than usual," she added, as she crossed the living room in the direction of the front door to the apartment.

"No problem at all, Julie," Lovett replied casually, not even rising from his armchair as the Frenchman had done. "See you next Wednesday, as usual?"

"Yes, next Wednesday as usual," she replied. "Goodnight," she added *à la cantonnade* as she closed the door behind her.

CHAPTER FOUR

S till standing, Canal turned to give his companion a feigned look of reproach. "You are not going to try to convince me that this magnificent example of feminine pulchritude is your housekeeper, now are you?"

Lovett shook his head.

"Or that she is your private masseuse looking after her towels and oils?" the Frenchman added, as he reseated himself.

The American shook his head anew.

"Vous les mettez à contribution maintenant, vos conquêtes?" the inspector joked suggestively.

"Of course not," the analyst replied dismissively. "There have been no conquests lately—I've been far too busy—and even if there had been, I certainly wouldn't put them to work in my office. Julie takes care of my correspondence and all my billing."

Canal evinced partial willingness to believe what he had in fact suspected—that, like many other psychoanalysts, Lovett worked out of his own home. Still, he could hardly pass up the opportunity to proffer a little *bon mot*, "All your billing and cooing too?"

"Just can't resist coming off as a birdbrain, can you?" the American riposted, always being one to give as good as he got.

"She is not the slightest bit enamored of you?"

"Perhaps the slightest bit, but it has never become a two-way street."

"She is not your cup of java?"

"No, not nutty enough for my taste," the analyst replied, sticking with the variation on the bean. "Rather too serious— Lord knows I've got more than enough seriousness myself! I prefer a woman who enjoys joking around and inspires me to be silly now and then."

"But not as a personal secretary, I see."

"It's hard enough to find someone competent—imagine requiring lightheartedness to boot!"

"Yes, just imagine …," Canal contemplated. "Speaking of joking around," he continued, "I'm trying to get a handle on the difference between these punning Clanians and Calanians of yours. Did the—"

"Not of mine! Perish the thought."

"No, indeed, I should not saddle you with such Clownians," the inspector agreed. "Would you say that the Clanians *practice* very differently from the Calanians?"

"Funny you should ask!" Lovett commented, laughing. "As far as I could tell, it was a humongous intellectual apparatus designed to draw theoretical distinctions without a difference, notional delineations that didn't make the smallest iota of a change in the use of the so-called therapeutic frame, the amount of time allotted to sessions, or the approach to interpretation."

"A purely academic exercise."

"Yes. It seemed to me that the most extravagant theoretical speculations could be entertained and even taken extremely seriously as long as they made absolutely no difference whatsoever in technique, which they all seemed to have fetishized."

The inspector rubbed his chin. "But the hardcore Clanians and Calanians must have thought it made a tremendous difference at the level of technique," he postulated, smiling.

"Indeed," his interlocutor admitted. "But for the life of me, I could never understand what it was."

"And if *you* could not understand it ..."

Lovett waited a few moments for the Frenchman to finish his sentence, and then proffered, "And if *I* could not understand it, then ...," giving the other rope enough to hang himself.

"That is all," Canal asserted. Then, seeing his friend's expectant look which indicated unanticipated touchiness, he added, "You know very well how the expression goes—if you could not understand it, then there was indubitably nothing to be understood."

Lovett wondered to himself whether it would have been more or less convincing had Canal left the "indubitably" out of his ostensibly complimentary statement, but was not given time to try out the alternatives for very long in his head, as the inspector asked a further question.

"So their theoretical divergence ended up interfering in the training of new analysts?"

"Boy did it ever! Had they confined their abstract debate to the forum provided by the Society tied to the Institute where the training goes on—"

"You mean there are two different organizational entities?" Canal asked, trying to keep all of this unfamiliar material straight.

"Yes, there almost always are at groups affiliated with APE. The Institute includes only a select few members of the Society who are deemed worthy to train future analysts. The Society is the more all-encompassing entity, since it includes all Institute faculty, *plus* everyone who successfully graduates from the training program."

"So the training program run through the Institute is not overseen by all members of the Society?" asked Canal, scratching his head.

"Things are organized a bit differently from city to city," Lovett replied, assuming the role of historian, "but in

New York the Society had no power whatsoever over the Institute and thus could not force the Clanian analysts who had taken control of the Institute to open the door to other approaches."

"So that is what eventually necessitated the Calanians' secession from the union? They were unable to have any say in the training of new analysts and were obviously never promoted to the status of training analysts?"

"Yes, the conflict over training analyst status was crucial, as has been true in virtually every instance of infighting at other institutes as well. The Clanians' refusal to promote even a single Calanian to the status of training analyst was devastating." Lovett paused to meditate for a moment. "Still, it's never quite that simple. Every institute is unhappy in its own particular way, as an Australian acquaintance of mine once put it, paraphrasing Tolstoy. I won't bore you with the details, but suffice it to say that, despite all the animus generated by the Clanians' monopolization of the Institute's training program, no split would have occurred had there not been a fiasco at the top echelons of the organization."

Canal indicated that he was all ears.

"The Clanian who headed the Institute engaged in a number of highly unethical maneuvers to publicly discredit and humiliate the Calanian who had managed to become director of the Society. More or less accurate reports of these maneuvers eventually found their way into *The New York Times, The Post, Newsday*, and—well, I think you get the picture."

Canal did. He was no stranger to the interplay between personal and power politics, attempts having been made to undermine him, stifle him, and sell him up the river often enough in the course of his long, variegated career. But rather than allow such painfully sordid memories to flood back over him, he requested a refill of *bernache* and, once served, observed, "So that brings us to the early nineteen-eighties and the founding of NIPPLES as a Calanian Institute within APE. That must not

26

be the end of the story, though, since you mentioned recent conflicts from around the time of your site visit."

"Quite right," Lovett agreed. "I had almost forgotten you were interested in those more than in the ancient history. Or rather," he said, rising from his armchair and beginning to pace around the room, "no doubt the ancient history does not rankle for me quite as much anymore as the recent events do—I probably just want to forget about the latest conflicts altogether."

Canal watched the analyst alertly as he trod back and forth across the living room.

Once Lovett had assembled his thoughts, he remarked that when psychoanalysts had nothing better to do than spend all their time fighting bitterly within their institutes for control over training programs, it was obvious that their patient pool was drying up. When everyone had a full practice, he continued, no one wanted to attend meeting after meeting and, apart from a few power hungry megalomaniacs, most people were willing to allow everyone a share in the teaching, training, and administration of the school. But when the number of patients dwindled to such a degree that analysts had to rely on the students who entered the training program to fill their practices, bitter struggles ineluctably began over who would be promoted to the lofty position of training analyst. The people in charge would naturally anoint only their pet graduates, and would help only their best friends and most assiduous sycophants earn a living by assigning new students to them as patients.

"The toadies were the most successful of all," Lovett exclaimed, stopping his pacing momentarily. "Real friends in such circumstances are hard to number, as you can imagine. Patronage is the analytic world's answer to the Mafia's system of mutual favors and obligations."

Canal raised his eyebrows at this and Lovett elaborated. "The more the younger analysts are beholden to you in the organization for honors, advancement, and patients, the more you tend to believe you can count on their support in theoretical disputes and internecine struggles. So you end up distributing favors to a select group of apparatchiks in the hope that when push comes to shove, they won't defect to the other camp."

"And what is the other camp we are talking about here?"

"Sorry, I got so caught up in detailing the horrible workings of the system that I forgot to mention how things evolved at NIPPLES!"

"I am sure there is much to criticize. Perhaps I can guess how they evolved ...?"

Lovett made a sweeping, inviting hand gesture in Canal's direction. "Be my guest," he said, "or 'be my worst,' as a practitioner whose work I know once put it, although the word *empire* was in there too, I'm sure."

Canal did not take this bit of bait, for it would have allowed Lovett to go off on a tangent about a practitioner whose work could hardly be very poetic given the sample he had cited. Instead, the inspector began, "Without knowing whether there were any outside influences on developments within the school, I would guess that over time two distinct camps evolved at NIPPLES: the traditional Calanians and the neo-Calanians. The neo-Calanians would no doubt have emphasized the later teaching of the theoretical leaders of the school, whoever they were, whereas the traditional Calanians, who had formerly no doubt made use of all stages of their leaders' teachings, found themselves defending primarily the early teachings against attacks launched by the neo-Calanians."

"Not bad," Lovett exclaimed, genuinely impressed. "Not bad at all. Naturally, this led to the formation of a middle group—it's a shame it wasn't based in Middlesex, New Jersey. Its members—"

"Let me guess," Canal begged and Lovett acceded to his supplication. "Although the third group's adherents initially tried to balance the early with the late teachings, they eventually became associated with neither the early nor the late, but with some fictive middle teaching whose boundaries were defined not by themselves but by the other two camps."

"To some extent," granted Lovett, "but they also try to remain open to other approaches to psychoanalysis than the Calanian, whether traditional or neo."

"Which must make them heretics to both the traditionalists and the neo-ists, *sit venia verbo*."

"It certainly does," the analyst concurred. "And why not let the ungainly word be pardoned since it is so well suited to the occasion? At any rate, each of the more extreme factions has taken to alternately soliciting the support of the middle group in its fight against the other faction and trying to force the middle group out of the Institute altogether. The middle group has ended up being a sort of pawn in strategic turf battles between the traditionalists and the neoists."

"A fine kettle of fish, indeed."

Giving nary a thought to this foreigner's uncommon command of folksy American colloquialisms, Lovett asked, "Did you, perchance, notice a strikingly beautiful woman who entered the club tonight just as we were leaving?"

The inspector attempted to shift gears and cast his mind back to their earlier change of locale. He recalled that the thought had occurred to him once they were in the street that he, for one, had never regretted the change in policy that allowed women to become members of the Scentury Club, adding as they did much needed color and liveliness. That brought back the image that had no doubt sparked the thought: an elegantly dressed blond woman wearing dark sunglasses despite the late hour. He nodded to his interlocutor, "Why do you ask?"

"She's a member of the middle group. Managed to start her training very soon after the founding of NIPPLES, around '84, if I'm not mistaken, before all the lines were drawn in the sand. She's the only representative of the middle group on the faculty, having been grandfathered in, as it were."

A loud knock came at the door to an adjoining room and the American stopped his pacing. He excused himself, saying that at this late hour it must be important, and expressed the hope that he would only be gone for a few minutes.

Amid sounds of doors opening and closing, Canal was left alone to marvel at Lovett's curious juxtaposition of a beautiful woman and grandfathering. "If she is a middle-of-the-roader," Canal thought to himself, "I wonder what the non-middling analysts down there look like ..."

CHAPTER FIVE

When the analyst returned, he provided no explanation for the intrusion—a private matter, no doubt, Canal reflected. Perhaps a paramour, though more likely a patient given what he had said earlier about having no time for conquests.

Ever curious, however, and rarely one to show much deference for the rather recent notion in Western history of personal privacy, the Frenchman asked, "One of your neurotics in crisis?"

"No," replied Lovett, manifesting that even if he had not spontaneously explained his ten-minute absence, he was in no way unwilling to, "one of my psychotics."

"Do you see many here at your home? Are not such people mostly seen in hospitals and specialized clinics?"

"Oh no, clinicians see tons of psychotics in outpatient settings. The problem is," Lovett added with a cross between a laugh and a humph, "most practitioners can't tell psychotics from neurotics—unless their patients report hallucinations and delusions that can't be overlooked—and end up treating all of their patients alike."

"Does that not get them into trouble?"

"It certainly does. Treating psychotics as if they were neurotics makes them incredibly anxious or angry, in the *best* of cases. In the worst of cases it can even trigger a psychotic break, leading to a fundamental change in people who had managed to live their whole lives without any hallucinations or delusions at all."

"You mean they were neurotic before and suddenly become psychotic due to something the analyst does?" the cagey Frenchman asked.

"No," replied Lovett who had heard the same question on many prior occasions. "To the untrained eye they may have appeared like virtually everyone else and may thus have been assumed to be more or less neurotic, like most people are. But to the trained eye—or rather *ear*—it's obvious that they are fundamentally different.

"Psychotics are not encumbered with repression, which makes their use of language and sense of humor different from neurotics'. The difference can be quite subtle at times," the analyst went on, "but once you learn how to detect it, you realize that a non-negligible portion of the population is psychotic, strictly speaking, even when not actively hallucinating or delusional. Most people don't realize that there are psychotics all around them—whether it's the guy who makes their favorite drink at the local coffee shop, the checkout girl at the grocery store, their next door neighbor, or their aunt."

Canal, who was far more knowledgeable about these things than he tended to let on, enquired, "Does this imply, as I have sometimes read, that they are capable of committing certain crimes neurotics might be incapable of?"

Lovett stroked his chin and replied, "Yes and no. Hollywood has contributed to giving psychotics the reputation of committing the most atrocious crimes and, granted, the most brutal and most serial among the killers *are* psychotic. But under certain circumstances, neurotics can commit serious crimes as well, the big difference being that neurotics often try desperately to undo a crime as soon as they have committed it or are racked by guilt to such a degree after the crime that they become virtually crippled in their attempt to forget what they have done and move on in life."

"I've heard that psychotics feel no genuine remorse afterward, even if they do sometimes show outward signs of shame in order to seem like other people. Whereas neurotics are often consumed by guilt, and feel they can never do enough to make up for their sin against a loved one."

"Quite right," the analyst concurred. "Neurotics often admire people who show no signs of inhibition or guilt—things they themselves feel plagued by, not even for real crimes, but simply for being the slightest bit mean to someone or even just *wanting* to be mean. The most neurotic need to imbibe large quantities of alcohol to overcome their inhibition to act aggressively, which then critically compromises their chances of successfully executing any sort of premeditated crime. In marveling at those who express aggression unrestrainedly without any form of liquid courage, neurotics fail to realize that such 'admirable' specimens are generally psychotic and couldn't feel inhibited or guilty even if they wanted to.

"The patient who came by tonight, for example," he went on, "has never expressed any remorse about attempts he has made to harm the various people he has confused himself with over the years. He had to serve some time on a couple of occasions more than a decade ago, but never once have I heard him say anything apologetic that had not been drummed into him by counselors he was made to see in prison—just a couple of phrases he had obviously learned by rote. You can tell because it's always the same ones."

Canal's ears perked up at this and he asked, "He confused himself with various people?"

"Yes, it's a common enough occurrence in psychosis, even though many mistake it for simple empathy or ordinary identification. In this case, and I'm speaking confidentially, naturally," Lovett said giving Canal a look of complicit silence regarding the matter, "the patient's name is Leon and he easily confuses himself with prominent people whose names closely resemble his own in spelling or sound. Many years ago it was Leonard Nimoy, later it was John Lennon, and most recently it has been Jay Leno, the late-night TV comedian. Leon heard Leno tell a joke on television tonight similar to one Leon himself had just heard and repeated, and the coincidence was too much for him—he was planning to meet Leno at the back stage exit knife in hand!"

Canal was impressed by the patient's lethal intent and made it plain that he was all ears.

"I've gained his confidence in the course of the treatment and convinced him to always call me or come to see me before he takes any kind of action," Lovett explained. "I always manage to persuade him that Leno has *not* planted a transmitter in his brain with which to appropriate his jokes and that Leno has *not* taken his rightful place in the entertainment world. Leon doesn't accept the notion of coincidence easily, always finding some special meaning in propinquity of every variety. To many psychotics, and even certain hare-brained analysts, there has to be some connecting principle between any two occurrences of a word, phrase, or joke in a short space of time, a secret and generally malefic link to which only he is privy. Which means that I have to work awfully hard to find other plausible explanations for such instances of 'freaky synchronicity.' But at least so far, so good," he added, lifting his glass to toast his provisional success.

Canal clinked glasses with him, and noticing suddenly that the analyst was showing clear signs of fatigue, asked him if he would join him at his home for breakfast the next morning. Lovett, who had hardly realized that he was on the verge of exhaustion, admitted he had had a long day and accepted the invitation gladly.

CHAPTER SIX

When the doorbell rang the following morning, Canal was deciphering some music at the piano and was at first reluctant to set it aside. But hearing his American friend's deep voice waft into the study from the foyer, he jumped up from the soft leather artist's bench and led Lovett into the dining room where Ferguson, his valet, had laid out an inviting table. Bright autumnal sunlight was streaming in through the large windows, whose curtains had been pulled back to multiply the effect of the morning dose of caffeine.

After enquiring whether the analyst had slept well and ensuring that he was provided with victuals, Canal excused himself for picking the analyst's brain so extensively, explaining that if he was to undertake this particular investigation, he needed to act quickly and yet could not act without some further information. "You told me about the tensions between the two extreme groups at NIPPLES and the middle group. I need to know something about how this affects their evaluation of applicants who wish to become trainees."

Lovett, who was looking refreshed—especially after being served a small stack of mouthwatering sweet potato pancakes and a cup of steaming Earl Grey tea by the ever attentive Ferguson—said that there was no need to apologize and explained, "When the NIPPLES Admissions Committee, which is dominated by the two sets of extremists, looks at new potential candidates, they immediately try to exclude anyone who appears to have eclectic interests so as to thwart the advancement of the middle group. The few potential candidates who are still interested in psychoanalysis at all, as opposed to the more flourishing fields of psychiatry, clinical psychology, and social work, have fortunately caught on to this and have learned to pretend they are exclusively interested in Calanian theory and practice."

"*Pas si bêtes que cela, ceux-là,*" Canal commented.

Lovett nodded in agreement. "More worrisome, though," he continued, "is the race to the bottom engaged in by the two extreme factions as they each try to bring in as many candidates of their own persuasion as possible. Instead of limiting the number of candidates accepted per year on the basis of criteria like quality of academic credentials or of prior clinical experience, each argues endlessly that candidates who show a marked preference for their camp should be admitted, no matter how inferior they may be intellectually or clinically. The factions obviously do so merely in order to swell their own ranks, and they have even taken to accepting a plethora of candidates who have been 'decouched,' as they say, elsewhere—in other words, booted out of other analytic training programs!" He sipped his odoriferous brew.

"Don't get me wrong," he went on, "like most of the other APE institutes, which are dying, they have been able to attract no more than two to four new candidates each year for over a decade now. But whereas the other institutes have about a fifty percent acceptance rate, which is already absurdly high compared to quality institutions of higher learning, NIPPLES has a ninety-nine percent acceptance rate. The kind of horse trading that goes on in that Admissions Committee is among the most shameful I have ever seen, the traditionalists agreeing to accept a neoist candidate only if the neoists admit a traditionalist in exchange, and vice versa." Disgust was plainly written on his face. "I felt obliged to tender my resignation when APE refused to do anything about it after we had made our official report as site visitors," he added dramatically.

"That must have sparked off quite a scandal," Canal surmised, after chewing silently for some moments.

"Not really," Lovett rejoined, pouring maple syrup on his pancakes. "No one is indispensable when the APE Executive Committee has decided to hush things up. Not a single committee member tried to stop me from taking my ball and going home," he added, smiling with a slight hint of bitterness in his expression. "I hear they even surreptitiously rewrote large portions of our report."

Canal continued to show that he was listening attentively, so Lovett, after swallowing a mouthful and gesturing his approval to the valet, went on, "The problem, you see, is that once candidates of dubious quality are accepted into a program, there's almost no will on the part of anyone in the Institute to kick them out. Each of them is paying somewhere between forty and sixty thousand dollars a year for tuition and training analysis and supervision, and the livelihood of numerous people in the Institute depends upon those funds. The same thing is happening at universities and colleges everywhere, of course, where *retention* is the new buzzword ..." Here Lovett interrupted himself to issue a warning, "I know what you're thinking, young man, but there's no point engaging in bathroom humor!"

Canal's matinal thoughts had not been ambling down that particular path. "So anality came to mind?" he said, jibing the analyst.

The latter smiled and resumed his earlier diatribe. "Institutions of so-called higher learning now consider themselves to be at fault when students flunk out. Students are held less and less accountable for their performance because instructors are strong-armed into passing students in order to keep their tuition dollars flowing. Teachers thus take ever less responsibility for guaranteeing the quality of the students they graduate from their programs. I remember one saying, 'He will never do us any harm—why don't we graduate him? We should have gotten rid of him long ago, of course, but let's graduate him already!'"

Lovett took another forkful of pancakes and smiled sardonically at this. "Naturally, those graduates end up becoming members of the Society and giving the Society and Institute a bad name since they do shoddy clinical work with their patients. And if that weren't bad enough, they often go on to blame the theory for their own inadequacies as clinicians and latch onto other approaches instead of the one they were trained in."

"So the factions end up cutting off their noses to spite their faces, if that is how the expression goes."

Both men mused silently as they chewed for some moments, contemplating the unintended consequences of the retention imperative. Canal, whose pragmatic concerns overrode his academic condemnation of the system (or was it condemnation of the academic system?), was the first to break the silence. "I wonder how I could best investigate the crime that occurred down there … It seems like it will be a complicated matter to gather information without raising suspicions on the part of one faction or the other. I may have to bite the bullet and go in undercover as a new trainee myself!" he added jokingly.

"Was it a very serious crime?" the American asked, looking up from his diminishing stack of hotcakes.

"I'm afraid so," the Frenchman nodded gravely. "A young, highly promising analyst-in-training, who was just about to receive an award for exceptional performance, was poisoned at one of their annual conventions."

In Lovett's astonishment, a morsel went down the wrong pipe and he began coughing.

After clapping him on the back a few times, Canal continued, "It was the kind of poisoning that led to death. It appears that there was a murder at the Institute ..."

"I've heard people say," Lovett commented after having cleared his throat, "that the training at psychoanalytic institutes was murder, but ...," his voice trailed off for a moment, "actual death by analysis? That's a new one on me! Not that I'm overly surprised—it had to happen sooner or later."

"How do you mean?" asked Canal, taken aback.

"In my experience, therapists' passions are, at least in many cases, no more moderate than those of other people. Analysts are perfectly capable of flying off the handle, slamming their fists on the table, and ranting and raving. The things that go on at meetings behind closed doors," he exclaimed, shaking his fingers up and down for emphasis. "You know, I've seen a few highly placed training analysts turn bright red and I could tell they would have liked nothing better than to throttle their so-called colleagues and trainees to within an inch of their lives!"

"It sounds like *your* presumption would be that she was murdered by her own analyst!"

"She? It was a woman who was murdered?"

"Yes, and she was apparently one of the youngest trainees NIPPLES had admitted in a very long time. They were positively thrilled to matriculate someone who, for once, was not already close to retirement age."

"I wonder if I know this trainee ...," Lovett pondered. "Did you catch her name?"

"Doreen. I was not told her last name. She was twenty-nine years old and apparently quite a looker. If I'm not mistaken, she was in the fourth year of the training program."

CHAPTER SEVEN

Early Monday morning a week and a half later, a certain Jean-Pierre Kappferrant, an established intellectual historian from Paris wishing to write a book on the origins and development of Calanianism, arrived at the modern building in which NIPPLES's offices were located. He had written the directors to request access to their journals, newsletters, course catalogs, memoranda, and fliers as well as permission to interview people at the Institute—whether on or off the record, as they liked.

His foreign credentials, like his alleged publications, were unfamiliar to the rival directors of the Institute and the Society. But as neither big cheese could see how a Frenchman could write anything that would conceivably help the opposing faction more than his own, both had agreed to allow him use of the joint library for up to a month. Their letter to him had nevertheless contained a cautionary caveat: although he was free to ask whomever he liked for an interview, they could not guarantee that any of the analysts or candidates would agree to speak with him.

Dressed in a black leather jacket, black slacks, pointy black shoes, and trendy looking rectangular glasses whose frames appeared to be upside down, smelling uncharacteristically of cigarette smoke, and carrying an exceedingly worn brown leather briefcase, Jean-Pierre Kappferrant rode the elevator up to the eleventh floor. He presented himself to the secretary behind the reception desk window as the French historian who was there to use the library.

The secretary, a somewhat awkward-looking man in his mid-thirties with curly red hair, massive quantities of freckles, and just the slightest trace of a lisp, had obviously been alerted to the foreigner's imminent arrival, for he immediately showed the Frenchman into the library. Henry, for that was his name, turned on the lights for the professor and explained that the librarian would not be in until later that morning—probably around noon. The visitor would, Henry surmised, have the place to himself for a couple of hours and had merely to come down the hall to Henry's station if he had any questions.

Once back out in the hallway, Henry Bowman, who had spent some time in Paris as a graduate student a few years prior, chuckled to himself at the stereotypically French attire, accouterments, and aroma of the *prof* with the funny name. He could now give free rein to the mirth he had quashed in the library when the man had knocked his briefcase on the floor as he took off his jacket and then dropped and almost stepped on his glasses as he bent over to pick up his briefcase. "I guess absent-minded professors still do exist," he said to himself as he remanned the reception desk.

The library was hideous, devoid of all natural illumination and flooded with harsh fluorescent light, as if to deter potential readers from venturing into it. The administration's powers of dissuasion seemed equally immanent in the complete absence of comfortable seating, all the chairs being hard wood straight-backed affairs. The remainder of the decor, if it could be called such, was cold and uninviting, smacking more of a nineteen-fifties science lab than of a modern bookshop with cozy cof-feehouse atmosphere.

Shaking off the chill it induced, Inspector Canal, alias Jean-Pierre Kappferrant, studied the lay of the land. Books by teachers at the Institute were prominently displayed near the entrance and he spent a few minutes glancing through them, connecting the names on their front covers with the vanity shots on their back covers or inside flaps. Realizing that if he were to get anywhere in this investigation he would have to avoid coming off like a complete ignoramus regarding Calanianism when he interviewed people, he had reluctantly picked up a couple of books on the subject before flying north to acquire his winter provisions of dark amber maple syrup, but had stopped reading after just a few pages, recognizing it as the kind of fodder likely to spoil his appetite and even his vacation as a whole. Still, he had forced himself to pour over a few of the early works in the field since his return from Knowlton and Westfield, and the names that got top billing at the NIPPLES library were not all utterly unfamiliar to him.

So these were some of the head honchos *qui faisaient la pluie et le beau temps*, he mused, who determined the fates of the Institute's candidates ... The inspector was well aware, however, that—just like in university departments—those who wielded the most clout often published little or nothing, spending all their time maneuvering and negotiating behind the scenes, consolidating one bastion after another. These powermongers he could discern only by perusing the Institute's internal documents, like minutes from meetings, newsletters, monthly bulletins, and the like.

Wandering among the stacks, he noted that whereas the spines of books regarding postmodern and post-postmodern trends in psychoanalysis were broken in numerous places, and their pages worn and heavily annotated, Freud's works appeared to have rarely been consulted, the editions purchased by the library in the early nineteen-eighties looking as fresh and crisp as ever. Despite Freud's warning against acquiring new ideas too quickly, even good ones, the new new thing seemed to have pride of place in the candidates' training.

Penetrating ever further into the recesses of the largish room and encountering nothing but monographs and journals, the inspector finally noticed large cabinets lining the wall at the opposite end of the library from the entrance. This must be, he speculated, where the internal documents were stored. And these were the kind he needed most to consult, for if he were to unmask an accomplice to Doreen's murder, he would need to know all about her likely friends and enemies at the school, all about her political and theoretical alliances.

His hypothesis that this was the administrative holy of holies was corroborated, he felt, by the fact that all of the cabinet doors were locked. Contemplating for a few moments whether he should ask the secretary if he could open them for him, he glanced nonchalantly around the room to ensure that there were no surveillance cameras and then swiftly and surely unlocked one of the doors with a small tool he extracted from his inside coat pocket. Should anyone ask how he had found those materials, he would simply assert that the first door he tried was unlocked and assumed everyone had access to them. Had the directors not, in any case, granted him access to most, if not all such materials?

Reaching into the cabinet, he quickly located just the kind of documents he was looking for: annual reports, minutes of Education Committee meetings, statutes and bylaws, the whole kit and caboodle. Within a few minutes, the organizational charts of the Institute and of the Society began to take shape in his mind, and he made a crib sheet for himself listing training analysts, instructors, and Education Committee members.

Returning the materials he had already consulted to the cabinet, he brought a small folder containing the minutes of the Admissions Committee over to the table at which he had initially set down his jacket and briefcase, and began flipping through them, looking for those pertaining to the entering class of which Doreen, whose last name turned out to be Sheehy, had been a part. Reading between the lines—for even minutes like these were censored to efface virtually everything that had transpired at the meeting should APE site visitors like Lovett ever take it into their heads to examine them—Canal could see that Doreen's acceptance had been vigorously promoted by William Watkins and George Peterson, both notorious neo-Calanians. So that was the young woman's camp, or at least self-professed camp.

The minutes included nothing about her qualifications or previous clinical experience—indeed, if the debate over the relative merits of *any* of the five applicants her year had been heated or not, the record showed nothing. One applicant's candidacy had been rejected after a very brief discussion. Two of the candidates appeared to have been trumpeted by the neoists and two by the traditionalists. Of whatever barter-ing had occurred during the course of the two-hour meeting (beginning and ending times *were* indicated in the minutes), the only trace was the conclusion: "Four out of five applicants unanimously approved."

"Unanimously, *mon oeil!*" Canal said to himself.

Rapidly scanning the hallway, the inspector reckoned that all continued quiet on the lower eastern front. A few patients were reading, or at least holding magazines in the waiting room, and Henry was staring at a computer screen at his post. The inspector returned the folder to the cabinet and began rifling around, looking for lists indicating which new analyst-in-training had been assigned to which training analyst. Find-ing no such lists, he picked the locks to the other cabinet doors and continued his search. Convinced that what he was look-ing for was not so sensitive that it would be kept elsewhere or shredded, he continued thumbing through every document he could find, checking his watch occasionally, until he noticed a small binder that appeared to have fallen behind one of the shelves and was wedged between it and the back cabinet wall.

45

Crawling halfway into the cabinet, he managed to fish the binder out and was overjoyed to see that it was exactly what he had been looking for.

Doreen had been directed to do her training analysis with Peterson, one of the two neoists who had pleaded her case for admission. A later page showed that once she had begun seeing patients under supervision, Watkins had been designated as her weekly supervisor. "All in the neo-Calanian family," Canal reflected to himself. And this Watkins must be the ex-husband of Wilma Watkins, Ponlevek's main suspect.

The Frenchman's next order of business was to locate the annual progress reports Lovett had told him institutes are required to prepare for each trainee. He had noticed no such folders thus far in his perusal, but looked again to see if they might simply have been labeled in some other less transparently obvious way. Noting that it was getting on toward noon, at which time the librarian was expected to arrive, he closed and relocked all the cabinets, figuring it likely that sensitive material like that was probably kept in the director's office files, not in the library.

CHAPTER EIGHT

auntering down the hall toward the reception area, Canal collided with a young woman coming out of what appeared to be a diminutive lounge, coffee mug, pad, and tape measure in hand. The majority of the hot liquid that splashed out of her cup landed, fortunately, on the linoleum floor and not on the professionally attired woman's clothing. After they had both apologized to each other profusely for not having seen the other coming, and had hastily wiped up the spilled fluid with paper towels and refilled her cup from the filtered coffee maker, the polite brunette chirped, "Sorry again— got to go measure my new office for drapes," and dashed off.

Returning his Parisian spectacles to his nose, Canal peered into the standing-room-only lounge for trainees and faculty the girl had popped out of. He made a mental note to spend some time there every morning and afternoon to meet the practitioners who constituted the local fauna around the proverbial water cooler, even if coffee klatch made more sense. Then he proceeded down the hall and sidled up to Henry's window. In the thickest French accent he could muster, he said, "Thank you very much for opening ze library for me."

"No problem," Henry replied, looking away from his computer monitor and examining Canal. "Did you find everything all right?"

"Yes I did, zanks. Can you tell me now where one can find a morsel in the *parages*?" Noticing the secretary's perplexed look, Canal corrected himself, "I mean, in the neighborhood."

Laughing up his sleeve at the Frenchman's word-for-word translation, if one could call it that, Henry proffered, "There is a place on the ground floor, but it's no great shakes—in fact, I'd recommend you steer clear of it."

"What would you recommend? I would love to disgust your typical American cuisine—I have not tried it since a very long time."

"Disgust?"

"That must not be ze right word. *Déguster*, let me see ..."

"Taste? Sample?"

"Yes, excellent," Canal cried, eyeing the man behind the window more closely now. "You speak French?"

"Je me débrouille tant mal que bien," the young man replied, performatively demonstrating the truth of his assertion.

"You speak very well," Canal commented encouragingly. "Have you passed time in France?"

"Yes, I spent most of a year in Paris during graduate school. But that was a while ago now and my French is getting pretty rusty."

"You could practice with me, perhaps?" Canal offered. By the eager smile on Henry's face, the inspector knew he had found the right angle.

"I invite you to lunch," he said peremptorily. "You will be capable of leaving soon?"

"I'm afraid I work straight through lunch."

"You don't eat? I can bring you something?"

The secretary silently held up a small brown paper bag that presumably contained his lunch.

"Bon, je vois," the purported professor parleyed. Not accepting defeat, however, he added, "I invite you to drink a glass later this afternoon, okay?"

"Bien volontiers," Henry exclaimed, quite pleased with the Frenchman's proposal.

CHAPTER NINE

After lunching as leisurely as is humanly possible at a nearby diner—Henry had given it an at least tepid recommendation—and spending a few hours skimming through Watkins's and Peterson's meager literary output, Canal followed the clinic secretary to a bar in the East Village, affecting to goggle at the people, stores, and buildings as though he had just recently landed there from another planet.

The people at the bar obviously considered themselves to be at the cusp of trendy, and the music was so loud Henry could comprehend precious little of Canal's crystal clear French, which he rendered deliberately simplistic for the occasion, aware as he was, as few who had not seriously studied foreign languages were, what kinds of idioms and grammatical constructions were difficult for non-native speakers. After an awkward drink, Canal proposed that they find a quieter locale. Henry avouched that he had assumed the Frenchman would want to sample—without having expected him to be disgusted by—the cutting edge of New York bohemianism and had steered him toward a place that he himself did not even like.

Ambling aimlessly, or so it seemed, in the general direction of midtown, Canal nonchalantly pointed to a calm looking restaurant—one he had heard good things about but had never yet tried, and at which he was quite sure he would not be recognized, for his current disguise was a thin one, being solely vestmentary—and proposed they go in there. The young man at first balked at the apparent priceyness of the establishment, but allowed himself to be talked into giving it a whirl.

Henry, as Canal learned, had been in the NIPPLES training program for the better part of six years now, attending part-time the first few years while he completed his Ph.D. in clinical psychology. Much to the New Yorker's dismay, he was still attending part-time in order to earn the funds necessary to pay for tuition, analysis, and supervision. He raved about his year-long stay in Paris, nostalgically recalling that he had managed to go over there to study French innovations in psychoanalysis while benefiting from university funding, something that had been sorely lacking since he completed his diploma.

Landing a position as secretary at the Institute's clinic had been something of a coup for him, for it not only paid him a salary but reduced his tuition drastically.

"What's more," he added somewhat cockily, after polishing off a first cocktail and taking a long draft of a second, "it gives me some leverage with the other students." By this point in the conversation, Henry had reverted to English, finding, as did many, that whereas his language skills had been unleashed after a couple of drinks back when he spoke French regularly, they unraveled altogether when he didn't.

"Leverage?" echoed Kappferrant with a questioning intonation.

His interlocutor was not sure whether the professor was unfamiliar with the term or simply wanted to know what kind of leverage. "Sway. Power, if you like," he explained, as he ran his fingers through his red curls.

Canal continued to look puzzled.

"You see, everyone is required to treat a couple of patients four or five times a week for at least three years before they can graduate. But plenty of patients drop out shortly before the three years are up, others rarely make it to sessions more than three times a week, and still others manifest a negative therapeutic reaction by not paying for the last six months or more of analysis! Any one of these will immediately disqualify the case." He knocked back the rest of his White Russian.

Canal could well imagine wherein lay the secretary's clout but, not wanting to appear too knowledgeable, confined his remarks to, "So you ...?" He simultaneously signaled the barmaid to refill his companion's glass, which she promptly did.

"So, since I am in charge of the date book, schedule, and accounts, I can sometimes make it seem that an invalid case was in fact bona fide, allowing a student's cases to be eligible for presentation to the Education Committee. That can potentially shave several extra years off a student's training period, thereby saving her upwards of a hundred thousand dollars in tuition and supervision."

Canal whistled at this. Then he articulated the single word, "Her?"

"Him or her," Henry explained, as though that were obviously what he had meant. Despite the dim lighting at the restaurant's bar and the young man's many freckles, it seemed to Canal that he blushed as he averted his gaze for a moment and started in on his third cocktail.

"Et donnant donnant?" Canal enquired.

The colloquialism sailed right over Henry's head.

"I think you say something like it iz only fair if I scratch back of yours, you scratch back of mine?" the inspector conjectured disingenuously.

Henry caught on now. "Yes, naturally I would expect something in return for such a *huge* favor."

"But what could students possibly propose in return?" queried Canal.

"Oh, this and that," Henry replied evasively. "When they made good on their proposal, that is!" he said vehemently, suddenly growing angry, his face reddening patently.

"*She* did not make good on *hers*?"

"She royally welshed," he cried, visibly enraged. Then, suddenly fearing he had let the cat out of the bag, he stumbled and bumbled his way into an explanation, the following words finally tumbling out, "The students I help pretend to wimp out like that at times ... just to mess with my mind. But it's all in good fun, really."

The lad was at this point clearly in need of solid sustenance to sop up the spirits, and the professor ushered him into the adjoining dining room and ordered dinner. Turning the conversation to Calanianism, Canal discovered that whereas Henry had applied to the program under the guise of fervent traditional Calanianism, he was actually more aligned with the middle group. This left him, as he said, between a rock and a hard place: none of the training analysts were from the middle group, and it had only been in his fifth year that he had been assigned a more like-minded supervisor for his clinical work.

The trials and tribulations of the non-aligned among the zealots soon came into focus for the inspector. Henry seemed to have been spared the worst recriminations and reprisals, for he had been careful enough not to flaunt his non-zealot colors until he was well along in the program. Others, who talked the talk throughout the interview process but refused to walk the walk the moment they started classes, had not, according to Henry at least, fared nearly as well as him.

In the cab on the way back to his fictive hotel, Canal recalled to mind the young man's momentary wrath, presumably sparked by his recollection that he had been unable to call in an enormous favor owed him by a woman in the program. As mild-mannered as he seemed, he was clearly subject, like most, to the sound and the fury ignited by a woman's scorn.

Still, the inspector reflected as the taxi pulled up in front of his building, a neurotic like Henry—at least that was Canal's working diagnosis—might foment a plan to take revenge on a woman who had welshed on a promise while he was enraged, but would probably temper it or even scuttle it once the initial passion had subsided, rather than carefully and methodically carry it out ... Or, had he acted in a fit of fury, he likely would have scrambled to *undo* the crime as soon as it had been committed. Yet there was no sign in Ponlevek's report of any attempt at undoing at the convention where the girl had been poisoned—no one had attempted to administer artificial respiration until the poison was out of her bloodstream, even though there would have been plenty of time to do so, curare taking quite a while to finish its victims off.

It was hard, moreover, to fathom why a neurotic like Henry would have knowingly aided and abetted the main suspect, the vengeful Professor Watkins, unless he had been having an affair with her. "Would that, could that make any sense at all?" the Frenchman wondered. Did the boy require two women at a time? And why would Wilma Watkins have egged Henry on to kill a rival if she herself had been engaging in a bit of *timélou, lamélou*? She would have *already* been getting even with her philandering analyst-husband ...

"Did Henry and this professorial carrier of curare even know each other?" Canal asked himself. He would have to find a way to feel the lad out about it, without raising any suspicions.

An unlikely accomplice at best, he reflected, but one who might easily have been persuaded by an anthropologist scorned, supposing they were just friends, to prick Doreen with what he believed was a ruffie or an aphrodisiac to coerce her to pay debts she seemed disinclined to reimburse in any other way. Perhaps he never even knew what he'd hit her with, having hoped to have an entirely different sort of effect upon her ...

CHAPTER TEN

Having spent a week at NIPPLES, Canal telephoned Peter Ponlevek on Friday afternoon proposing that they meet to compare notes. The NYPD Inspector was, as it turned out, expected for dinner by his fiancée, FBI Special Agent Erica Simmons, at her apartment and managed quite easily to get Canal invited along too.

Ponlevek had initially been none too pleased with the Kappferrant stratagem Canal had settled upon, primarily because the Frenchman had both concocted and acted upon it without consulting him (Canal forbore revealing that he *had* consulted about it with Jack Lovett, Ponlevek's analyst). The man in blue had been a bit nervous that he would blow Canal's cover by greeting him in his usual mechanical manner upon encountering him at the Institute, but, perceiving the potential wisdom behind the ruse, had consented to avoid all contact with NIPPLES for the duration of his elder's inquiry. This might give Canal a freer hand, the analysts and trainees potentially opening up a bit and presenting less of a united front once the "heat" disappeared.

Simmons, always a smart dresser who knew how to set off her wavy brown hair to good advantage, was attired less professionally when she greeted Canal warmly at the door than she had been when working on the case of Mayor Trickler. She was looking particularly radiant and wearing a seasonally pumpkin-hued sweater and chestnut-colored skirt, her shoulder-length hair flowing freely rather than being pulled back as it often was during assignments. As the inspector handed her the spray of flowers he had picked up on the way over, he noted with satisfaction that she was holding an apron in one hand, suggesting that this aficionada of haute cuisine most likely had not contented herself with ordering takeout for their evening repast.

Canal was happy to hear that the society of so many New Yorkers with their inelegant intonations had made no inroads upon her slight Southern drawl and to observe that she and Ponlevek appeared to be rather more at ease with each other than they had been when last he had seen them together, well over a year before.

Ensuring that the Frenchman was comfortably seated and supplied with something other than Ponlevek's perpetual Coke, Simmons excused herself, saying that the dishes on the stove required a moment's attention. For his part, Ponlevek was tickled pink to have the inspector witness his affianced felicity.

"Protein?" asked the NYPD inspector in response to comments the Frenchman made as they began conversing about what Doreen's fellow trainees at the Institute had said about her.

"No, *protean*," Canal repeated, "as in multiform, able to take on many different appearances, hydra-headed."

Simmons returned from the kitchen at this point and joined them. "Who's hydra-headed?" she asked. "I hope you're not talking about little ol' me."

"Certainly not," Canal replied, winking at her. "We are talking about Doreen Sheehy, the girl who was murdered. Seems to have charmed the pants off all the male faculty—one of those girls who elicits something from a lot of men, employing her looks and a certain pleading, longing way of talking to them that appeals to their rescue fantasies. A chameleon of sorts, I suspect, incredibly adept at reading others' soft spots and playing up to them. Even one or two of the female faculty fell for her act," he remarked. "She had a knack for giving each of her teachers the impression that she agreed utterly and completely with his or her insights and views, allowing her to perform quite well for three years in the program without doing much work."

"That must have made her well liked in the student body," Ponlevek ironized.

"Two of the students I took out for lunch found it laughable, feeling that it confirmed their cynical views of their teachers' perspicacity—"

"Or rather lack thereof," Simmons quipped.

"Indeed," exclaimed the Frenchman. "A third however, Rosalynn, was clearly quite infuriated by it. Luckily for me, she had no patients scheduled the day I took her out for a chat. And she selected a rather nice Japanese restaurant for lunch, where they serve an especially fine sake I know."

"What a surprise," Ponlevek cried. "Booze seems to be your favorite investigative method."

"It does loosen the tongue, as does good food and good company," Canal retorted, feigning pique. "Beats sodium pentothal, in any case. So, early on in the lunch, this Rosalynn tells me she became close friends with Doreen right from the first day of the program, even though she was some ten years older than Doreen, and the two became inseparable during the first couple of years. Their fellow students apparently joked that the two were joined at the hip!

"But two hours into lunch," Canal continued, "and well into a sizable bottle of sake, Rosalynn reveals to me that Doreen's ignorance and manipulation of faculty members had recently gotten on her nerves so badly that she had called an old friend of hers who had gone through the same doctoral program in psychology as Doreen at Dickleigh Unfairson. You know what she discovered? *Je vous le donne en mille."*

"She never went to that graduate school at all?" conjectured Ponlevek, ignoring the French interjection.

"Her name wasn't Doreen?" hypothesized Simmons, following suit.

"Her name *was* Doreen and she *was* enrolled in that graduate program, but she was dismissed for ethical violations and never completed her degree. Rosalynn calculates that Doreen matriculated in the NIPPLES training program just a few short months after her expulsion from Dickleigh Unfairson, in no way leaving enough time to finish her degree at another school."

"So this Rosalynn," Simmons speculated, "may be the only person who knows that Doreen faked her way into the Institute's training program, fudging her CV to make it look like she had received her diploma."

"Don't they run background checks on these people before agreeing to train them as psychoanalysts, or at least authenticate their sheepskins?" queried Ponlevek, incredulous that such a professional training program could lag so far behind the checks required for New York's finest.

"Either they dispensed altogether with verification or else her neo-Calanian supporters were so eager to have a young and promising student like her, who could potentially carry their banner for decades to come, that they hushed up her dismissal. The internal conflict between the traditional Calanians and the neo-Calanians is so intense that almost anything is possible."

"So even if this Rosalynn never told anyone else at the Institute," Simmons concluded, "a few people on the Admissions Committee might possibly know."

"They might," Canal conceded. "Rosalynn's level of annoyance suggested to me that she had already gone to the faculty about it and was infuriated to see them sweep it under the rug, or else had threatened Doreen that she would reveal it."

"You would think dat Rosalynn would be the one to get knocked off, then," Ponlevek deduced, scratching his head, "not Doreen, and that Doreen would be the killer."

"Unless Doreen acted cocky with Rosalynn, telling her it wouldn't matter one way or another—they loved her too much to ever kick her out of the program," Simmons postulated.

Ponlevek's eyes opened wide. He was first surprised at the hypothesis and then concerned that such a thought could even have occurred to his fiancée. Did it imply something about her, he wondered. Could only women fathom the psychology of other women?

His reflections were interrupted by the Frenchman agreeing with Erica: "Right. Such an attitude might have driven Rosalynn to take matters into her own hands … She was quite jealous of Doreen's academic success in the program, which far outstripped her own—primarily because Rosalynn refused to kiss ass, if you will excuse her French. You know how it is in these classes—if one student gets a very high grade, someone else inevitably gets a lower grade so the class average comes out in accordance with some preset standard."

Simmons nodded, recognizing the kind of "gerrymandering"—as she liked to think of it, coming as she did from a short line of politicians—that went on in her own master's program.

"I got the sense that Rosalynn was initially fascinated by Doreen's ability to attract male attention, and even hoped to ride her coat-tails to success with the men at the Institute, expecting to glean some dribs and drabs of admiration through her association with Doreen. But after a while, she seems to have become enraged at Doreen for all the men she had wrapped around her little finger. I was also able to ascertain," Canal went on without pausing, "that Rosalynn knows your anthropologist, Watkins's ex-wife. Apparently met at a few NIPPLES social functions and became friendly—though just how friendly, I don't know yet."

CHAPTER ELEVEN

Simmons directed the two inspectors to the dinner table and brought out the autumnal appetizer, pumpkin soup. "Who were all these men," she asked, "that Rosalynn believed Doreen had wrapped around her little finger?"

The Frenchman, ever concerned to place etiquette first, protested, "We must not bore you all evening talking about our investigation—I am sure you have enough cases of your own to keep you bored to your heart's delight."

"Very kind of you to think of that," replied the Southerner, "but I find your investigation refreshing after all the number crunching mine involve," she being a specialist in fiscal fraud.

Canal helped her into her chair and then seated himself where she had indicated. "There are always plenty of men in such programs to entrance," he observed.

"Everyone I spoke with agreed she was a very likable girl," Ponlevek retorted. "Nobody said anything about her wrapping people around her little finger."

"I suspect you spoke primarily with the very people who were so wrapped."

"These pros oughta be able to tell when some chick is faking it," Ponlevek objected, finishing his soup.

"Can you?" Canal asked Ponlevek, winking at Simmons.

Ponlevek's jaw dropped uselessly, so his fiancée answered for him, "Peter can never tell when someone's faking because he's an open book himself. He couldn't fake anyone out to save his life!"

"Except maybe Olivetti," Canal jibed, referring to Ponlevek's boss whom Canal knew well.

"Enough about me," Ponlevek finally objected. "We were talking about Doreen. I'd have thought a shrink should be able to see through an act, if there was one."

"You might think so, but whether headshrinker or not, most people see only what they want to see."

"But look, I talked with this one analyst—I think Peterson was his name—who raved about Doreen, saying she was a fine student and the sweetest trainee they'd had in the program in a long time."

Canal put his spoon down even though he was far from having finished. "That, you see, is what should immediately set off alarm bells for us."

"Why is that?"

"Because Peterson was Doreen's analyst," the Frenchman replied and it was clear from the expression on Ponlevek's face that he had not had the foggiest.

"Your analyst shouldn't think you sweet?" asked Simmons curiously, although apparently somewhat crestfallen.

"After three years of analysis four or five times a week, one would suspect—so I have been told—that an analyst's impressions of his or her analysand would be slightly more nuanced and complex than Peterson's were of Doreen, if what he told your fiancé is to be lent credence."

"You mean he shouldn't like her anymore?" asked Ponlevek, diving directly from nuance to the nether regions.

"I hear there is sometimes a sort of honeymoon period during which the work goes very smoothly and both analyst and analysand are enthusiastically engaged in it. But sooner or later, the action of repetition and its ineluctable repercussions on the transference generally lead to a moderating of enthusiasm on both parts."

Ponlevek's features bespoke blatant befuddlement.

"To put it more simply," Canal proposed, relenting, and keeping in mind that his interlocutors were both in the early stages of analysis themselves, "as interested as analysts remain in working with each analysand, they eventually tend to find each analysand trying in his or her own way."

"Trying what?" asked Ponlevek.

"Trying *tout court.*"

"As in presenting difficulties in the course of the treatment?" proposed Simmons.

"Precisely," Canal nodded to her gratefully.

"So let me get this straight," Ponlevek plodded forward. "If this Peterson didn't find her the slightest bit trying after three years, you're saying that ..." Canal encouraged him to go on with a facial gesture. "She wasn't really doing analysis with him?"

CHAPTER TWELVE

"**M**ust you really wear these hideous clothes, sir?" asked Ferguson, as he came through the breakfast nook on Saturday morning with the Parisian professor outfit that he had prepared at his employer's request. "I'm afraid they make you look quite the ...," the tall, balding butler of indeterminate age trailed off, apparently unable to find a suitable epithet or one pronounceable in polite society.

"Cad?" offered Canal. "Scoundrel? *Fripouille*?"

"Something like that," the valet replied, shaking his head regretfully. "Would not some other form of attire—"

"I am afraid not," the inspector cut in. "If I am to be convincing in my role, I have to dress the part. Sartorial sensibilities will have to be strained a little longer."

Returning to his cappuccino, Canal re-examined the photographs of the crime scene that Ponlevek had lent him the night before, showing Doreen, the large round table at which she had been poisoned, the placement of the other tables in the giant convention center ballroom, and so on. As no one else was, for obvious reasons, still seated at the table in these police photographs, Canal had asked Ponlevek who had been seated at the same table with the dead trainee. The New Yorker had given him a copy of the seating chart drawn up by the convention organizers.

They obviously had no confirmation that people actually sat at their assigned tables, for despite an organizer's best efforts, people often switched seats with other people, removed the cards telling them where to sit, and even destroyed the seating cards of people assigned to their tables that they did not want to have to look at for three hours. There was apparently no documentary evidence of who sat where, there having been no photographer present during the banquet. Even if there had been, that still would not have told them who was at which table at all times, Canal reflected, since people have a tendency at these affairs to jump around a little, eating the main course at one table, and lingering over dessert at another next to people they would rather talk to, or feel a need to make a show of wanting to talk to ... He made a mental note to discreetly ask people at the Institute who was sitting where and when.

Ponlevek had even mentioned that there had been dancing at the gala, so different people might well have been getting up and sitting down throughout the better part of the meal, which could hardly help them narrow down the field of suspects, easily giving many different people the opportunity to stumble and "accidentally" stab Doreen with a little needle.

Henry, the man to whom Doreen had promised everything and given not even Arpège, was officially seated at the next table over from Doreen's. Canal wondered what, if anything, might have set him off that night, since it sounded like he had been doing her favors for quite some time and she had probably been putting him off, always promising that she would reciprocate soon. Perhaps he discovered something about her at the convention dinner itself or just prior to it that he had not known before, Canal mused. Something related to her love life, no doubt. Perhaps she had been affecting to be unattached and it came to light that she was actually rather seriously attached?

He scrutinized the seating chart again and noticed a name opposite Doreen's at her table. By now he recognized most of the names at the table—they were almost all faculty members at NIPPLES—but who was this Thario fellow, he asked himself. "L. Thario," he read silently. "Maybe it's not even a fellow," he thought next.

It was customary to seat a guest's consort directly across from the guest at a table, as opposed to alongside the guest, Canal recalled, so as to oblige couples to mingle with their fellow diners. Lord knew few people were aware of, much less followed, the rules of etiquette these days, he reflected, but perhaps this L. Thario was Doreen's significant other whom no one at the Institute had ever known anything about before.

The person who opened up the RSVP envelopes and drew up the seating chart would likely have known Doreen was bringing someone with her at least a few days in advance. That could have been a staff member other than the clinic secretary, but then again it might well have been Henry, Canal figured. Shocked that she was coming with a consort, Henry might have googled this person or searched through the phone book and found a Lucifer Thario living at the exact same address as Doreen. Putting two and two together, Henry might have reckoned that, if she was living with someone, he was probably *never* going to collect on the amorous favors she kept promising—unless, that is, she was not in her right mind thanks to a little subcutaneous aphrodisiac … Why, though, would he have given it to her with her significant other present?

Taking another sip of cappuccino, Canal scanned the seating chart anew in search of Rosalynn's name. "Now, what was her last name?" he asked himself. Hergé's Dupont and Dupond flashed through his mind, and he suddenly recalled that it was Thompson. Peer as he might, however, he remained unable to locate her anywhere in the ballroom.

The inspector recalled his conversation with Ponlevek and Simmons about the possibility that Rosalynn had reported Doreen's dismissal from her Psy.D. program for ethical violations to the NIPPLES faculty and that it had been ignored.

Had she become livid and unsociable to the point of refusing to even make an appearance at the gala dinner?

Different scenarios presented themselves to Canal's mind, one after the other. Rosalynn might have confronted Doreen directly and told her to withdraw from the program or else. Depending on how desperate or conniving Doreen was, she might have threatened in return to take down the whole Institute with her, making a public scandal of the Institute's lack of vigilance regarding the clinicians they unleashed upon an unwitting public. NIPPLES would then be discredited and Rosalynn would find herself graduating from a tainted training program …

That might sound excessively desperate to some, but Canal had known people in educational, entrepreneurial, and governmental settings who were ready and willing to take the whole damn place down with them if necessary. In any case, it might have sufficed for Doreen to simply threaten to do so for Rosalynn to have backed off.

Which would have given Rosalynn all the more reason to join forces with Wilma Watkins, he reflected. But then why had she not gone to the gala?

Maybe Doreen knew something about Rosalynn that made it impossible for Rosalynn to rat Doreen out to the faculty—a past criminal record Rosalynn herself might have had, drug addiction, alcoholism, or patient problems of some kind, things she might have been keeping from her analyst and supervisor. Canal knew that most trainees felt under great pressure to hide from their analysts aspects of their past or present that they believed would lead to an unfavorable evaluation, which might prevent them from graduating. They fit themselves into a Procrustean couch, instead of waiting to be forced into one, striving in the consulting room, as Doreen had in the classroom, to say exactly what they believe their guides wish to hear. He had even heard that things were so absurd in most North American institutes that trainees often did a first analysis "for the school"—not revealing anything to their assigned training analyst that might jeopardize their chances of receiving the Institute's blessing—and a second analysis later for themselves with someone they could really talk to without it endangering their careers.

Officially, their analysts no longer participated in the decision to let them graduate or not, as they had in past decades, but officiously, loose lips still sank ships.

Training rarely works the way it is supposed to on paper, reflected Canal, shifting uneasily in his chair, thinking of his own years of so-called higher education. He made a mental note to ask Ponlevek to run background checks on Doreen and on Rosalynn too. Then, recalling the marvelous *Daube à la provençale* and flaming crêpes suzettes Simmons had served up during the previous night's meal, he added a note to ask Ponlevek to get him invited over for dinner more often—that was, after all, his preferred form of remuneration for assistance on cases.

Was Henry the assassin, with or without Wilma Watkins's assistance? Was L. Thario the proximate cause of the young man's fury? Or were Rosalynn and Wilma Watkins in on it together? *"Que de questions sans réponses!"* the Frenchman exclaimed to himself. If he was going to get some answers, he would have to talk with Professor Watkins herself, not just with her possible accomplices. But try as he might, he could think of no plausible way of approaching her without raising her suspicions.

As a consultant to NYPD Inspector Ponlevek, he would probably be met by her with stonewalling, since she knew she was suspected by the police of having poisoned Doreen. As Parisian Professor Kappferrant, an attempt to interview her regarding Calanianism would, in view of her recent divorce, appear quite lacking in sensitivity.

He could, he reflected, pretend to be a professor of South American archeology or anthropology, but he was afraid his meager knowledge would give him away too quickly. Perhaps he could convince someone hitherto unconnected with the investigation to pretend to be a student interested in her area of expertise? Or interested in the predicament of women in academia, the thought occurred to him out of the blue, which might open the door to questions about marriage and divorce? Maybe he could talk Erica Simmons herself into pretending to be a journalist or a graduate student writing an article. Given her interest in different cuisines, perhaps she could even pretend to be a writer on culinary topics related to Amazonian gastronomy, assuming there was such a thing ...

CHAPTER THIRTEEN

The fall weather was exceptionally fine on Monday morning and Canal found the idea of perusing dusty volumes at a library unpalatable, even if it was in the hope of waylaying one of the analysts on his NIPPLES list. Two weeks indoors was all he was willing to endure, and so rucksack in tow, he set off for New Jersey. His plan was to find a park to hike around for a few hours and to end up at the Stanhope Union Cemetery—where Doreen had been buried, according to the police report—in the vague hope that inspiration would strike owing to a complete change of pace and decor.

The sky was blue, the air was crisp, Canal mused as he drove, and the colors of the autumn leaves, although hardly rivaling those of northern New England, were lovely, even if the parison struck him as trite.

Temperatures in the sixties suited Canal's hiking temperament to a tee and he lost track of time as he gamboled from one crest to another in Allamuchy Mountain State Park, the terrain transitioning from wooded hillocks to lakes and back again.

The waning four o'clock sun saw him receiving directions from the cemetery gatekeeper to the recent grave site, and wending his way among the trails and alleys to the spot indicated, which was not yet marked by a tombstone.

The inspector surveyed the nearby gravestones, noting the proximity and progression of Doreen's extended family, which included such unexpected names as Pappen and Heimlich, and eventually seated himself on a nearby bench to meditate— or was it doze?

Images of endless Appalachians aflame with orange and red maple leaves passed before his mind's eye, and he saw fiery hues reflecting in the glassy waters as if he himself were gliding lightly in a canoe across the surface of a long finger-like lake. His head must have fallen forward, for he awoke, as it were, with a slight start and a snort, and a voice coming from very close by apologized for having disturbed his slumbers.

The voice belonged to a young man of around thirty, dressed in black jeans and a leather jacket, with a trendy hairstyle and diminutive diamond earring.

"I accidentally knocked over my bouquet," he explained, gesturing to the flower arrangement he had scattered over the mounded earth.

"So I see," Canal replied sympathetically, without overlooking the suspicious-sounding "accidentally."

"Funny place to get some z's," the young man commented. "Makes me want to cry, not sleep," he added, fighting back some tears, of which he had apparently already shed a fair number judging by his bloodshot eyes.

"You knew zis person?" Canal enquired in his habitually thick French accent, as he gently tapped the part of the bench to his left with the palm of his hand, silently inviting the young man to have a seat next to him.

"Yeah," he replied, standing a bit shakily, "you might say that." Slumping heavily down on the bench at the furthest distance possible from Canal, he added, "We've been together for, like, three years—I mean were together." Sensing imminent waterworks, he changed the subject, "You must not be from around here—visiting some long-lost relative?" His eyes surveyed the many tombs visible from where they sat and, before

Canal could formulate a reply, he remarked, "Not a bad place to spend eternity, if you have to, I guess. Though I'd rather be ..."

"You would rather be ... ," Canal echoed with a questioning intonation.

"I don't know," the young man said evasively. The inspector gave him all the time he needed to go on. "Annihilated in a flash, leaving no trace behind. Nothing for people to, like, snivel over or decorate with flowers."

"You would not want someone to bewail your disappearance?"

"Nah, what's the point?" the other replied cynically, even as he wondered at the stranger's unusual turn of phrase. "Dude, you're, like, *gone* anyway."

"I am gone?" Canal asked, as if he had not understood the American colloquial use of "you," even though he knew only too well that the shift to the generic inescapably dissimulated a double meaning, one which included the interlocutor far more than the British "one." Given his age, he realized he might well appear to this boy as a father or indeed grandfather figure, whom the lad might be all too happy to have gone from his life.

The young man perceived no such subtleties or ambiguities. "Not you, man, me! If I don't make my mark in life, I, like, don't want people lamenting the loss of my *untapped potential* after I'm gone," he exclaimed, the two highlighted words being pronounced by him exactly as he had, no doubt, all too memorably heard them stressed by a parent or teacher. "If the only trace I'm gonna leave is a tombstone, I might as well, like, just end it all now."

"You are bemoaning your own unfulfilled dreams in advance?" Canal asked cryptically. "As if you were already sure they would never be realized?"

The young man eyed Canal narrowly, not entirely sure what he was getting at. "I can see the writing on the wall," he proffered eventually. "I never finish a single song. And if it weren't for my band mates, I, like, wouldn't even play at the benefit concerts they manage to get us booked at." He looked down at the ground between his feet now. "At the rate I'm going ..." He broke off this thought. "And now with Doreen gone too ..." He set about blubbering again.

"Doreen was her name?" Canal asked in an empathic tone of voice.

"Yeah." He continued to stare at the ground.

"What was she like?"

"She was wonderful," he replied, perking up a little, raising his head. "Not at all like me—even when she didn't know where she was headed, she was, like, 'I'm gonna get there before everybody else,'" he exclaimed, full of admiration. "Supported me through thick and thin, paid for everything unselfishly."

"A real pearl!" Canal commented approvingly, even though he wondered just how unselfish her supporting him through thick and thin had in fact been. By paying for everything, had she not kept him treading water, going nowhere—maybe even under her thumb? "Pretty too?" the Frenchman asked.

"Gorgeous!" the would-be musician replied. "A real knockout—I never figured out how a loser like me wound up with a girl like her ... ," he added and then lapsed into thoughtful silence. A cool late-afternoon wind began to blow and the two zipped and buttoned up their coats.

"You make it sound like you were the sole beneficiary of your relationship—did she not get anything from you?"

"Not much, I'm afraid," he replied mechanically. After a few moments, though, he added, "Actually, she got quite a bit more than I thought she did." He suddenly flared up. "Turns out she, like, used me in her training ..." He broke off, apparently fuming now.

"Training?"

"Yeah, she was training to be a shrink," he said, and seeing Canal's feigned incomprehension, added, "a psychoanalyst."

A couple in their twenties walked by arm in arm, and the young man instinctively looked the female half of the couple up and down intently.

"Hmm," Canal grunted reflectively. "Is she the girl I read about in the papers?"

The young man nodded, glad not to have to retell the whole story. "Pretended I was, like, a patient she had been seeing four times a week for three years," he exclaimed indignantly. "Reported to her supervisor about her supposed work with me every week—I guess to get advice about how to handle me!"

Canal could scarcely believe his ears. *"Nom d'un nom d'un nom!* How did you find out?"

"Total fluke," he replied, shaking his head almost in disbelief. "I was put at Doreen's table with a bunch of bigwigs at one of these humongous affairs analysts have during their conventions, and for whatever reason we got on the topic of the music scene in New York. I made some rude comment just to mess with them and this random geezer turns to me and says, 'That reminds me of something Doreen told me one of her patients said—I don't know if she ever talks with you about them—he's quite a case!' I don't think anything of it at first until he starts repeating almost word for word things I, like, said to Doreen just the week before."

Canal's eyebrows were about a mile high, stunned as he was by the girl's combined mendacity and audacity.

"I was, like, dude! What da …" the would-be musician cried and then interrupted himself before shocking the foreigner's presumed sensibilities.

"I can imagine."

"I was ready to kill her then and there!"

Canal's eyebrows appeared to rise higher still, if such were possible. "Who would not have been?" Canal echoed the lad's sentiment.

"She once told me she was gonna lie, cheat, and steal her way to being the most trusted analyst in New York, and I guess she, like, wasn't kidding! No one could ever have accused her of having elephantiasis of the conscience. It caught up with her, though—she got hers," he added, shrugging his shoulders.

Canal's features evinced perplexity.

"I mean she, like, got what she had coming to her," the young man said, finding another idiomatic expression—impenetrable to the average foreigner—which he felt conveyed what he wished to express. "Not through any help of my own, of course—don't get me wrong," he said hurriedly, as though suddenly realizing that what he had said might easily be misconstrued. "Somebody must've felt even more used by her than I did!"

"You mean her death was not ..."

"From natural causes?"

Canal shook his head. "I thought I read something about medication complications."

The young man shook his head in turn. "That was just a story they made up for the papers."

"Did she not have some kind of medical condition?"

"Not unless you call a passion for prescription pain pills a medical condition!" the American replied, laughing. "Healthy as a horse."

"Prescription pain pills? What was she taking those for?"

"The pain of existence, I guess. Depression, anxiety, panic, whatever you want to call it. She had benzos, codeine, SSRIs, you name it—a veritable arsenal."

"Was she not in analysis to learn to cope with existence?"

"Doreen didn't buy any of that ... ," the young man retorted, leaving out the epithet that was to follow. "I don't know what she was telling the analyst dude she was paying the big bucks to ... She just went to see him because she had to—it was, like, a requirement. She made up half of what she told him, I'm sure. Drugs were her lifeline. Everybody had, like, a chemical imbalance, she always said."

"Why did she want to become a psychoanalyst if she did not believe in psychoanalysis?" Canal asked, incredulous.

"Cushy job, easy money—what more could you ask for?" his interlocutor replied as if it were self-evident. "Told me it was so easy, what with patients doing all the talking and analysts being instructed not to ask any questions, that she decided to withdraw from her Psy.D. program"—Canal's ears perked up at this—"and go straight into analytic training. Figured she could doodle or snooze through half her sessions and still be considered to be doing awesome work!"

"A rather cynical perspective."

"She thought the stuff being done at the Institute was so lame that when I asked her once if she, like, felt I should go into therapy, 'cause I was particularly down, she tried to get me to take some of her happy pills instead."

"You did not want to?"

"Never trust anything synthetic, I say," the would-be musician explained. "I prefer the natural stuff, like weed."

"Weed?" Canal echoed, playing up his straight-off-the-boat foreigner status.

"Yeah, you know, like reefer, grass, Mary Jane." Perceiving no recognition in his interlocutor's eyes, the young man finally proffered, "Marijuana."

Canal nodded. "So the medical condition mentioned in the paper ... ?"

"Total fabrication. Anything to, like, avoid a scandal," he exclaimed irreverently. "It was poison," he asserted impressively. Then, seeing Canal's grave face and feeling his own tone in the last couple of minutes did not match the solemnity of the site, he explained, "I never would have gone that far, naturally. I mean I was angry and everything at her for using me as a case, but when you think about it, it was actually kind of rad—uh—funny. There she was, talking about me every week to this geezer down at the Institute," he added, plainly flattered.

He shifted positions on the bench. "It was off the hook, really! The dude seemed to be *totally* in love with her, the way he went on and on about her at the banquet, and all the while she's telling him about me, her real boyfriend, making him jealous and all hot under the tool belt. I think she got a real kick out of messing with the old fogies downtown!"

"You are not the kind to be jealous?"

The young man bristled at this. "Well, yeah," he replied defensively, "when there's something to be jealous about. But I never worried about the Viagra crowd—she just led them on." Seeing Canal's meditative expression, he asked, "You think I should've been worried about them?"

"How would I know? I never had the pleasure of meeting the girl. Everyone tells me she was a fine student and a delight to work with."

"What do you mean? Who's everyone?"

"I am over from France researching the history of Calanianism to write a book about it," Canal explained, "so I have been talking to several of the students at the Institute and a few of the analysts as well."

If the young man was surprised by the coincidence, he did not show it, retorting instead, "The students must take you for a fool then, 'cause I can assure you they pretty much all hated Doreen's guts. Except for the guys, naturally—they were all crazy about her."

"She seemed to interest herself in them?"

"Yeah," his interlocutor replied, the odd reflexive not bothering him a whit, "I caught her messing around with a couple of them, and half a dozen other guys as well, sometimes friends of mine. She had a dangerously roving eye!"

The inspector scrutinized the young man keenly. "What did you do about it?"

"Put her in her place and beat some sense into her, when I had to."

"That would do the trick?"

"For a while, at least. Then I'd overhear her talking to someone, follow her around a little bit, and catch her hanging with some random dude."

"Hanging?" Canal echoed, trying to get a handle on the circumference of the word's signification.

The would-be musician was nonplussed at first. Then he seemed to grasp the purport of the question. "No, not hanging like this," he explained, squeezing his neck with his hand and sticking his tongue out. "Getting together with, hooking up with, spending time with."

"And in the United States of America that is equivalent to cheating on someone?"

The young man was taken aback, as if he had been accused of making Doreen's infidelities up, but the inspector had formulated his question in such an abstract, sociological way that he found it hard to take direct offense.

"There's but one step from the dining room to the bedchamber," he cried, unintentionally misquoting Napoleon. "When a girl starts making up lies, when she tells you she is working on a course project and you find her having a candlelit dinner with wine at some guy's house ..."

"Maybe *he* wanted to seduce her, but *she* was just using him to do the coursework for her?"

"You don't wear short skirts, fishnet stockings, and high heels to do homework."

"It sounds like *she* did," Canal remarked nonchalantly. "Did you not imply that she was very adept at leading men on?"

"Things went a lot further than that," he exclaimed, jumping up. "Believe me, she wasn't the kind to hold anything back. There were times I could've ..." He lapsed into silence and then began anew, "A guy knows when he's being diddled."

Canal relented at this point, having elicited much of what he wanted to know, and not wishing to push the young man so far he would never speak to the inspector again. "It must be difficult," he sympathized, "when one's girl diddles everyone, as you say. One can never know when she is telling the truth or pulling the wool over one's eyes."

"Oh, I could tell," his interlocutor retorted. "Where there's smoke there's fire. I got pretty good at sniffing 'em out after three years."

"Yes, I can imagine," Canal said, rising to his feet. "Three years is a long time …" Under other circumstances, the Frenchman would have been inclined to quibble, saying that where there's smoke, there's more likely to be a smoker than a fire, but things being what they were he let it go. Taking a last look at the freshly mounded grave site, and observing the rosy hue of the thinly filleted, fish bone clouds veiling the setting sun, he proffered, "Can I depose you anywhere? I have a borrowed car that is parked just outside the cemetery."

The young man's face, which had grown somewhat tense and somber during these last exchanges, brightened visibly at this point and he accepted the offer gratefully. "That'd be awesome, thanks," he enthused. "It took me three buses to get out here."

Walking side by side toward the exit, Canal said, "By the way, I call myself Professor Kappferrant, Jean-Pierre Kappferrant." So saying, he extended his hand to the other.

The young man, raised in a part of the world where the tradition of shaking hands upon being introduced to someone had lost a good deal of steam in recent decades, awkwardly took Canal's hand and clasped it weakly. "My name's Lou, Lou Thario."

CHAPTER FOURTEEN

Having dropped Lou off at his apartment building in the East Village and made a mental note of the address, Canal could at last drop his act of being a foreigner who has not the slightest idea how to get around the tri-state area. He had kept having to remind himself to ask Lou for directions, but since Lou did not have a car, he was often clueless as to which road to take, which lane to get in, and so on. To keep up the charade, the inspector had taken a few turns he knew were wrong, even though they led to traffic jams, just because Lou recommended them.

Keeping the conversation going had also proved something of a strain for the inspector, contrary to his usual experience, because the American had few interests apart from a form of contemporary music about which Canal knew little, even if he was willing to learn. And because, like many an American these days, Lou showed a total lack of curiosity about his interlocutor, asking only, in the course of an hour's journey together, what kind of car it was and who had lent it to him. The theories of human development Canal had known and not loved proposed that younger people were generally more curious about the world and interested in a wider variety of things than older people. He sincerely hoped it was not true, because if it was, he hated to think what today's thirty year olds would be like at sixty!

If there was something other than music Lou genuinely was interested in, it struck the Frenchman that it was in finding Doreen guilty of cuckolding him. Based on everything Canal had heard thus far, the girl sounded like an incorrigible flirt who led men on to extract favors from them, but who rarely if ever delivered on the hopes she had raised in her admirers. Was Lou so insecure about his own qualities, so convinced he was worthless, that he had concluded she must necessarily prefer every other man to himself? Or was he himself the one with the "dangerously roving eye"? His libidinous scrutiny of the obviously attached female who had passed them in the cemetery had not escaped Canal's lynx eye—perhaps he was the one having affairs behind Doreen's back, whether in the flesh, virtually, or in fantasy alone ... "Is that not, after all, the way it so often is?" Canal reflected. "One reproaches one's partner for the very things one is most guilty of oneself."

This Lou Thario might well have a good deal to reproach himself for. The more he cheated or thought about cheating on Doreen, the more he reproached her for cheating on him. The harder it was for him to suppress his sexual interest in other girls, the more enraged he became at her. He was not the kind, Canal felt, to exact punishment on himself for having such thoughts, to force himself, for example, to stay with her all the more brutally the more he wished to leave her. No, his was a projective nature, not a self-punishing one. His reaction the moment Canal had brought up the topic of jealousy was telling. The stronger and crazier the jealousy, the stronger the self-reproach.

Just how far this modern-day Othello had gone, the inspector could not be sure, but he fully intended to return of an evening to talk with Lou's neighbors to ask what they knew, to see how far his arguments and fights with Doreen had gone, to gauge the level of murderous passion between them. Those

84

comments he had made about putting her in her place and beating some sense into her might have been the braggadocio of a Milquetoast, but then again …

"Even a milksop," Canal reflected, "can be pushed too far sometimes if a woman points out every single way in which she thinks he is a wimp. In fact," he mused, "poison might well correspond to the approach that would be preferred by just such a *chiffe molle* …"

Stopping short at a light that had changed unexpectedly, the inspector suddenly realized that he had neglected to explore any possible connection between Lou and the primary female suspect. It now occurred to him that the aspiring musician had motives enough of his own to do his girlfriend in. And he had, by his own admission, been present at the gala dinner where she had been poisoned. Still, curare was hardly to be found in your local convenience store or medicine chest …

CHAPTER FIFTEEN

Friday afternoon found Canal examining some papers at the large round table in the NIPPLES library. He had long since made the acquaintance of Jocelyn Josephs, the institute's librarian, a svelte, attractive woman in the prime of life who had been married to one NIPPLES director after another, seemingly gravitating wherever the locus of power lay, despite an apparent lack of doctrinal passion one could clearly call her own. Her interest in the school's different factions seemed to be confined to the various personalities involved, whom she worshipped or reviled depending on the tide, the season, or whatever it was that happened to determine her passions— Sagittarius rising and Jupiter in Gemini, if her own explanations were to be lent credence.

Canal, *pour en avoir le coeur net*, as he told himself, had checked the sign in the lobby to make absolutely sure that the psychoanalytic school he was investigating was indeed called the New Institute for Psychoanalytic Psychoanalysis and not the New Age Institute for the same, but his eyes had not deceived him. He wondered if one could find a single psychoanalyst who openly embraced astrology in all of France—he, at any rate, could not recall having heard of any. American eclecticism never ceased to amaze him.

But seated at the table in the steely cold library, Canal's thoughts were elsewhere. He was pondering his list of accomplices: Henry, the clinic secretary, who had done Doreen some signal services that had never been paid for; Rosalynn, the best friend turned vindictive classmate; Lou, the insanely jealous boyfriend ... He had sent Ponlevek to question Lou and Doreen's neighbors, several of whom had mentioned hearing loud fighting, dishes breaking, doors slamming, and the like coming from their apartment. The woman who lived directly below them had called the police on a couple of occasions, but no signs of physical abuse had been detected and the couple had been let off with a warning each time.

Beating sense into Doreen had apparently not been Lou's approach to her supposed infidelities after all, but then what had? Getting even by multiplying his own infidelities? Or planning a way out of the situation that he was not able to handle in any other manner? Canal was inclined to see the shock he had received the night of the NIPPLES ball as nothing more than the straw that broke the camel's back, not as the actual motive—more the detonator than the explosive charge itself.

As for Henry and Rosalynn, nothing new had yet come to light. He tried to imagine plausible scenarios for each of them ...

His cogitations were interrupted by the arrival of a well-put-together blond woman who smiled at him and asked if he minded if she joined him at his table. Promptly standing and shaking her outstretched hand, the inspector returned his trendy spectacles to his nose and recognized the newcomer as the analyst from the middle group he and Lovett had passed some weeks before as they left the Scentury Club.

She, fortunately, had heard that he was Professor Kappferrant and had sought him out in precisely that capacity. "I certainly hope you will find time in your busy schedule to interview me," she effervesced, smiling at him without any touch of timidity. Canal could detect no trace of a New York or even a

88

New England accent in this shapely blonde's voice—was she perhaps, he wondered, from Chicago?

Word of his interviews had spread throughout the NIPPLES Institute and Society by this time, and as fastidious as his questions were purported to be, no one seemed to want to be left out of the history he was writing.

"You are ...," he said disingenuously with a questioning intonation.

"Caroline Drago of middle group fame."

"Yes, of course. I have heard a good deal about you and fully intended to ask you for an *entretien*, a meeting."

She smiled at the ambiguous word choice.

Looking around the room, and noticing that the librarian had disappeared into the back and appeared to be on the phone, Kappferrant proposed that they speak there and then. Drago opined that sensitive topics were better discussed elsewhere, and suggested that they retire to a nearby coffee shop she knew.

CHAPTER SIXTEEN

The coffee shop was a quiet one and the lighting at the corner table Drago had selected after they had placed their order was muted. The professor made a show of taking out a notebook and opening it to a fresh page, and then asked her the same question he had asked everyone else, "How do you see the evolution of Calanianism over the years?"

If she were disappointed that he had gotten down to business so quickly, she held her cards close to her chest. "As far as I can tell, Calanianism itself hasn't changed a bit, at least since the early nineteen-eighties."

"No?" Canal cocked an eyebrow. "What do you make then of the different factions that have developed themselves within the school?" he asked, deliberately employing the French reflexive verb form.

"The clash of the Titans," she replied sarcastically, her hands dancing into a great crash above the table. "A couple of swelled heads saying to each other, 'This town ain't big enough for the two of us!'" she added in an affectedly deep voice.

Canal could not help but laugh at this gun slinging, Wild West characterization of splits within the Institute.

"Watkins and Josephs couldn't share their inheritance—"

Both of Canal's eyebrows rose at this last word, so Drago explained volubly, "Together they had convinced APE to let them break away from the Clanians who controlled the New Yorkers' Psychoanalytic. But jointly inheriting NIPPLES, an APE-accredited institute, was more complicated than they had apparently expected—each of them was dead set on being top banana, neither being the kind to shrink from a fight. Theoretical differences had to be found by each of them to justify the establishment of separate power bases."

"So in your view," Canal commented, impressed to hear such a no-nonsense perspective on the history of the school compared to the piles of transparent rationalizations he had heard from the other analysts he had interviewed during the past week, including Watkins and Josephs, "it was not a question of the narcissism of small differences, but rather the fabrication of small differences to justify narcissism?"

This formulation seemed to tickle Drago's fancy, for she laughed merrily as the waiter placed their coffee before them. "Which explains why high theory, Realpolitik, and backstabbing are inextricably intertwined at institutes like ours, disparaging gossipmongering probably being the absolute favorite pastime of every analyst."

"Perhaps of every non-analyst too?"

"Yeah, maybe," she conceded, smiling. "By the way, we say 'the narcissism of minor differences,' not small differences," she said, gently but unapologetically correcting the historian's English.

"How much difference is there between small and minor?" Canal asked ludically.

"Four letters," Drago replied, without missing a beat.

"*Rondement calculé!*" Turning back to his questions, the professor asked, "What make you thus of your so-called third group?"

"A ragtag, motley crew including anyone who couldn't or wouldn't get behind Watkins or Josephs. In fact, there's a kind of pilgrimage made by many who train at the Institute—they start out at either extreme, since they have been the only portals into the Institute for some time now, and whether they eventually become disaffected, disabused, or disenfranchised, they eventually gravitate toward the middle. If things go on like this much longer ..."

"The silent minority will one day become the vocal majority?" Canal proposed an end to the sentence she had let lapse.

Drago pinched her mouth and smirked slightly at this. "You never know."

"And then you would become *calife à la place du calife*—how do you say that in English?" he affected to wonder aloud. "Caliph in the place of the caliph?"

"The new big kahuna in town?" she proposed uncertainly, her college-acquired knowledge of French never having included the likes of *Iznogoud*.

The self-professed historian nodded.

"I notice you aren't writing anything down," she remarked. "Does it mean this is all off the record or do you have some sort of photographic memory?" she asked teasingly, examining Kappferrant narrowly over her cup of coffee, which she now sipped gingerly.

"I do have something of an *audiographic* memory, having trained myself in mnemonic techniques invented in antiquity, *memoria rerum* and *memoria verborum*. I associate each segment of an interview with a part of a city or a room in a house. As you tell me your views, for example, I imagine walking in my mind's eye from one room in the house to another."

"Be sure to let me know when you reach the bedroom," she bantered as if nonchalantly, continuing to sip her coffee.

"Were we," Canal queried, in no wise having missed the overture in her request, "about to explore terrain that you wanted to keep off the record? Something about you becoming the new big kahuna?" he winked almost imperceptibly at her.

The American was both annoyed at this seemingly effortless parry and impressed by the professor's ability to stay on topic and read between the lines.

"Kahunas without *cojones* do not seem to be very highly appreciated at the Institute," she observed pointedly. "Unlike you Frenchmen, I don't think they can handle a woman on top," she added, glancing at him keenly.

"One would think that with a name like NIPPLES, one would find greater appreciation for the fairer sex there."

"One would, but—well, I'm sure you've heard what happened to one of our sex …"

"You mean you think …"

"Speaking strictly off the record," she began, shooting Kappferrant a significant look, "I think she was an unscrupulous, unsophisticated upstart who was incredibly adept at gaming the system. But there have been male students who have done much the same thing without getting it in the neck the way she did."

"So you suspect one of the male faculty members?" As no immediate response was forthcoming, he asked, "You suspect *all* of the faculty, therefore, as in *Murder on the Orient Express*?"

Drago surveyed the café's patrons carefully before continuing. "I suspect Peterson and Watkins above all."

"They are the major misogynists at the Institute?"

"No," Drago replied, "no more misogynistic than anyone else. But I think they both suddenly realized Doreen had been toying with them big time for years."

"Suddenly?"

"At the annual gala. I overheard them talking while I was searching for an earring of mine that had fallen behind the cash bar."

Canal wondered how her earring might have wound up in such an unlikely location, but forbore to interrupt.

"I was crouching in a spot," she went on, "where only the barman could see me and I figured it was safer not to

94

show myself once I realized who they were and what they were discussing. It was toward the end of the evening and, their thirst not adequately quenched by the alcohol that had been served during the meal, the two of them had evidently decided to have a couple of stiff ones together at the cash bar."

Seeing that Kappferrant was listening attentively while he drank his coffee—although she could not tell that he was wondering whether she too had been insufficiently sated by the libations proposed by the organizing committee and had had a few cocktails herself at that very same cash bar—she continued, "My auditory memory is probably not as good as yours, but as I recall, Watkins was boasting to Peterson that he was on the verge of having an affair with a beautiful young thing, planning to whisk her off to Tahiti. He revealed that it was for this very girl that he had ended things with his wife of thirty years a few months earlier. These particulars coincided too completely with things Peterson, who was Doreen's analyst, had heard Doreen say on the couch for him not to warn Watkins as a friend that if it was the girl he thought it was— and he must have made some sort of hand gesture, pointing to her at her table or on the dance floor—he knew for a fact that she was just using him and had no intention whatsoever to run off to Tahiti with him."

"*Là!*" ejaculated Kappferrant. "That must have hit him pretty hard—a true low blow."

"It certainly did, although he refused to believe it at first. But Peterson provided so many corroborating details that Watkins finally seemed to acquiesce. He didn't exactly take it as a friendly caution, however," she added, "but decided to deal Peterson a blow to the soft, fleshy regions in return, divulging to him that Doreen's clinical technique owed nothing to Peterson's sit-back-patiently-and-wait-for-the-patient-to-bring-things-up style. He declared she was the most active trainee he had ever worked with in all his years of teaching.

"Watkins claimed that he had encouraged Doreen to be a little bit more active during the first few months he supervised her, feeling she had gone too far in embracing Peterson's notion that one mustn't ask the patient questions about things she doesn't spontaneously bring up. Can you believe anyone would propound such a view?" she exclaimed sarcastically.

The professor uttered but three words, "*Credo quia absurdum*," indicating to Drago that, like Tertullian, it was precisely because it was so absurd that he believed it. No fiction writer, he felt, no matter how gifted, could have invented the ridiculous practice of playing dead if Peterson had not "discovered" it himself.

"Watkins averred," Drago went on, "that Doreen had then gone from one extreme to the other. She went so far in the other direction that he had spent the past two years trying to stop her from asking patients about anything and everything she was curious about—whether it was pumping them for information about movies, about restaurants, or about what other people said about Doreen herself. And he had had to work hard to prevent her from uttering everything that popped into her head as though it were a profoundly worthwhile interpretation.

"He told Peterson in no uncertain terms—Peterson, a man who has always taken great pride in producing new analysts in his own image—that Doreen had obviously concluded he was a wuss who didn't have the balls to interpret anything and who she could manipulate at will. She was clearly just going through the motions of completing an analysis with him."

"It iz difficult to imagine an analyst taking such news calmly. One might expect him to wish to kill the messenger."

"He did—the two of them almost came to blows over it at the bar. Then they suddenly grew quiet, and later I thought I even saw them leave the banquet together."

"Still," protested the self-styled professor, "even if they had decided to join forces against the girl who had duped them both instead of killing each other, I do not see how they could have procured themselves poison within a few minutes—unless one of them had already projected to kill somebody."

"What are you talking about?" Drago asked, baffled. "The girl was poisoned the next day at the luncheon."

Now it was Canal's turn to be befuddled. "The next day? It was not at the gala on Saturday night?"

"Of course not. I don't know who you've been talking to," Drago admonished, "but either your audiographic memory is not all it's cracked up to be or someone's been feeding you false information. Some historian you'll make if you continue relying on sources like that!"

Canal wondered to himself whether Ponlevek had been mistaken or if they somehow could have gotten their signals crossed so thoroughly, so much of so-called communication being miscommunication ... Cognizant, however, that such details should not be of terribly great import to an intellectual historian of Calanianism, he swiftly returned to an earlier topic.

"It would be fair to conclude, then," he summarized, "that you do not believe the New York Calanians are about to elect a woman director? What about the Calanians elsewhere?"

Drago noted the brisk return to professorial business and reckoned that she had perhaps teased the Frenchman just the teensiest bit too much. "Are there really any Calanians worth talking about other than in New York?" she asked wryly.

Her interlocutor feigned confusion.

"You will soon learn, Jean-Pierre—I may call you Jean-Pierre, mayn't I?"

The professor nodded.

"You will soon learn that we New Yorkers recognize the existence of nothing beyond the suburbs of Long Island, Connecticut, and New Jersey. If it isn't happening in the Greater New York Metropolitan Area, we don't pay the slightest attention. Many consider it snobbery on our part, but I say, 'Don't hate us because we're beautiful!'"

Canal, who tended to listen in several registers at the same time, was struck by this formulation that he had never given a moment's thought before: were we being asked to put aside our silly jealousy of their beauty, or were we, rather, being asked to weigh their beauty in the balance more heavily than our pre-existing hatred for them? He decided, however, to leave that for a later day's reflection—along with the nascent line of thought about how those not born and raised in New York like Drago often become the most thoroughly New York-centric—and to try a different tack. "It iz true, you are beautiful," he said enthusiastically, purposely equivocating between the individual and collective *you*.

This was clearly more along the lines of what Drago, who was willing to take the collective along with the individual if need be, had hoped to hear from the dashing Frenchman. She extracted a card from her purse and pressed it into Jean-Pierre's hand. "I'm having a Halloween party tomorrow night—you will come, won't you?" she entreated, standing and edging toward the exit.

Canal was a bit surprised by this abrupt *lever de la séance*, as he thought of it later, and required a few moments to mentally consult the Saturday social calendars for his dual identities: lunch with yet another morose training analyst for the one, then afternoon tea with Professor Sheng and his wife for the other. Unless his audiographic memory were playing tricks on him, he *was* free Saturday evening. By the time he signaled that he would come, the American was halfway out the door.

Slightly dumbfounded, Canal studied the card she had left him. "Costume *de rigueur*," it read. Now where in tarnation was he going to find a decent costume the day before Halloween? he wondered to himself. Everything worth wearing would be long since rented.

Drago's thoughts as she exited into the busy street were of a rather different order. Certain of the handsome Frenchman's expressions and gestures had reminded her of someone she had seen before, but she could not put her finger on where or when. It struck her as odd that he would look familiar to her, since she had been to France but once, and that had been only for a few days during a whirlwind tour of Europe she had made with a group of her fellow students during her junior year in college. Still, she had the uncanny feeling that she had seen him, if not actually met him, somewhere far more recently than that ...

CHAPTER SEVENTEEN

City University was located in a part of Manhattan where Canal had often ventured, though rarely accoutered in the way he was this Friday afternoon. Dressed and perfumed as Jean-Pierre Kappferrant, he wandered the giant campus-in-a-building on Fifth Avenue in search of the office of Dr. Wilma Watkins, having placed a call to Ferguson regarding his need for a costume posthaste.

His scruples about the indelicacy of asking the recent divorcee to discuss the history and development of a school of psychoanalysis so closely tied to her ex-husband had evaporated when it became clear that virtually everyone at the Institute knew her at least a little bit and that she had therefore very likely gotten wind of the presence of a French scholar in their midst. Although Erica Simmons had been willing to unofficially play the part of a writer on culinary topics and interview Watkins about Amazonian cuisine, the FBI Special Agent did not feel sufficiently abreast of the details of the case to inconspicuously steer the conversation in the desired direction.

Canal had toyed with the idea of assuming yet another disguise, that of a so-called non-traditional student seeking advice about going back to school for an upper-level degree in anthropology, but had been concerned about getting his different personas confused and about the possibility of running into this Wilma Watkins again in a different context—in the company of someone she knew at NIPPLES, for example—in the course of the investigation.

She had not exactly welcomed him with open arms when he had called her to schedule an appointment, but had finally agreed to let him try his luck at finding her available during her Friday afternoon office hours.

He waited patiently on a metal folding chair outside her door for some twenty minutes, as an assortment of students of different ages and widely ranging appearances trickled in and out of her office. The inspector was quite shocked when she finally opened the door for him—she looked nothing like the pictures the librarian had shown him of her that were hanging on the walls at the Institute, some of which had been taken as few as six months before. A vast transformation appeared to have occurred in the discreetly graying, stodgily dressed woman in the prime of life captured in the photos taken at NIPPLES social functions.

The specimen before him now had short, spiky, grayish-white hair, at least six earrings running the length of each ear, a tongue piercing, and studded black leather armbands on her rather untoned looking biceps. This contrasted sharply with the sort of Hawaiian muumuu she was wearing, a loud print sleeveless dress of no determinate shape, which descended all the way to her sandaled feet.

"Cat got your tongue, laddie?" she opened the conversation sarcastically. "You weren't expecting the ex-wife of a prominent psychoanalyst to look like this?" she asked, pointing at herself from toe to head, as if to ensure he missed nothing of the complete tableau.

Canal, whose astonishment had been more perceptible than he had thought, said, "I must admit that it is hard to find a resemblance between yourself and the pictures Jocelyn Josephs was showing me not more than an hour ago."

"Well, don't let appearances fool you—I'm just as ornery and cantankerous now as I was before!" She examined the Frenchman's face keenly to see if her attempted witticism had been lost on him.

It had not. Kappferrant smiled and thanked her for her willingness to speak with him, indicating that whatever she said could be on or off the record, as she liked. He removed a pad and a small recording device from his worn leather briefcase and she responded, after gesturing to him to have a seat and closing the door, "I have nothing to hide."

Attuned as he was to double entendres, the inspector wondered momentarily whether this did not in fact indicate a wish on her part to show all, no matter how unsavory, rather than constituting a declaration of innocence, but he set that train of thought aside for later and began the interview.

"Given your background, I thought I might ask you first about any possible link between ze earlier work by anthropologists like Geza Roheim and Claude Levi-Strauss and the psychoanalytic founders of Calanianism."

Watkins appeared to be at least superficially impressed by the question, for which she had a ready answer. "You could still find some cross-fertilization between psychoanalysis and anthropology back in the days of the Clanians, but by the time Calanianism came into being, it had become a one-way street. Anthropologists continued to read plenty of works by psychoanalysts—and they still do—but analysts stopped reading virtually anything outside of their own narrow little field."

The Frenchman nodded and Watkins went on, "Used to be that analysts considered psychoanalysis to be just one small part of the broader humanities and social sciences, with a great deal to learn from literature, sociology, archeology, and even history," she added, glancing at the self-proclaimed historian. "Nowadays, they'd rather think of it as an independently constituted field on a par with sciences like biology and physics."

103

Her interlocutor appeared to be taking notes at this point, so she continued, "I think it's the competition with psychology and psychiatry that has been making analysts lose their way. Psychologists and psychiatrists have always pretended their work was scientific, squeezing it into some kind of pre-existing scientific framework, no matter how trumped up or unsuitable for studying human beings. Freud, for all his lip service to the scientificity of psychoanalysis, never neglected its sister disciplines and even considered them indispensable for the training of clinicians. But do any psychoanalytic institutes today teach literature, linguistics, anthropology, or sociology?" Watkins asked with an admixture of indignation and despondency. She suddenly heard her rhetorical question differently due to the presence of a Frenchman. "Well, maybe in your country they still do … Certainly not over here."

"Not even the traditional Calanians?" queried Kappferrant.

She shook her head.

"Neither the neo-Calanians?"

She shook her head again.

"What about the middle group?"

"Don't be fooled by their supposed tolerance and pluralism—they're no less analysis-Nazis than the rest of them."

"Where do your own alliances lie, assuming you have any?" the Frenchman asked, his pen poised to immortalize her position.

"I'm sure people think I should always have been a fervent supporter of neo-Calanianism, because my ex-husband was, and should now revile it because of what has happened …"

Kappferrant regarded her expectantly.

"But much as I loved my husband, I never actually understood the *momentous* difference between traditional and neo-Calanianism. As intensely as I abhor virtually everyone at the Institute, I neither like nor dislike Calanianism any more than I always did. It's never been at the crux of my own work in anthropology, curiously enough."

"Have you always detested the people at the Institute?" the historian enquired. "Or just since the divorce, if you don't mind my asking."

"Always!" she replied vehemently, "Always, always. How could anyone not detest them? Ever since William, my ex, trained at NYPS, I've hated everyone and everything associated with analytic institutes. Academia is antiseptic and asinine and whatever you like, but it can't hold a candle to analytic training in the stupidity department, based on what Willy went through. You want to just *kill* everyone involved!"

"Who do you resent the most there? Is there some group— the faculty, the training analysts, or the Education Committee— you think is most at fault?"

"The students."

Kappferrant cocked an eye at her.

Seeing this, Watkins went on, "No contest! The students are responsible for the reproduction of the idiocy of the system. If they refused to go along with it, if they refused to play the game, something would have to give and some semblance of sanity might ensue—I said *might*," she added emphatically. "There's no cure for the naïveté, if it isn't outright masochism, with which they allow themselves to be tormented year after year! It's like they're asking for it, like they're just as caught up in the whole stupid power thing as their teachers are."

Kappferrant cocked the other eye. She was on a roll now and he did nothing to impede it.

"And the female students there are just as bad if not worse than the male students. I generally expect more sanity from women than from men—maybe just a prejudice on my part," she added as an aside, pursing her lips at the historian. "But somebody's gotta put a stop to their machinations. At least in our Ph.D. program here, I can still fail a student. It isn't easy, granted, because the other professors tend to get up in arms. But at the Institute, no one ever fails, no one ever drops out, everyone graduates—the only way out is death!"

Her flood of words suddenly dried up, as if she were surprised by the extravagance of her own conclusion.

Canal examined her features carefully out of the corner of his eye, all the while pretending to be jotting down notes. Her mouth twitched, and this faint tic was followed by a slight spasmodic convulsion of a muscle near her left eye. The woman had something on her mind or conscience ...

CHAPTER EIGHTEEN

"That must've been some interview you had with the Dragon," a female voice exclaimed as Canal returned to the NIPPLES library late Friday afternoon. He had come in search of a manuscript to which he had found an intriguing reference earlier that day.

The voice belonged to Jocelyn Josephs who, at this tardive hour, had let her long blond hair fall out of its tidy bun. The attractive librarian was seated at a table munching a rice cake, and was essentially admitting through her utterance to having spied on the Frenchman from the back room while he spoke and then left for coffee with Caroline Drago a few hours earlier.

Drago's comments on the predilection for loose talk among those in the analytic world were fast finding confirmation.

"The dragon?"

"Caroline Drago, the maneater. I'd watch my step with that one, if I were you."

"My step?" Canal reiterated, as if failing to comprehend. With a glance he asked if he could join her at the table, to which she assented with a sweeping hand gesture.

"People joke about my three husbands at the Institute," Jocelyn remarked, "but I can't hold a candle to Caroline—she goes through more men in a weekend than I could in a month of Sundays!"

Canal affected to calculate the length of time designated by a month of Sundays and then gave her a feigned appreciative look. "*Praemonitus, praemunitus,*" he recited, but seeing in her eyes no recognition of the Latin proverb, added, "I believe you say something like, 'Forewarned, forearmed.'"

She winked at him as if to indicate that he had grasped her intent, without bothering to supply him with the missing *is*.

"Where does she find all zese men?" Canal enquired.

"Oh, hither and thither," the librarian replied, snickering. "She appears to have a great many connections in the art and music worlds, and is constantly going to parties, benefit concerts, charity balls, and the like."

The historian appeared to contemplate this.

"And when she runs out of men in New York," Jocelyn added just the slightest bit maliciously, "there are as many conventions and congresses in other states and countries as one could possibly wish to attend. I've been to plenty of them, and believe you me, there is no lack of men, whether attached or unattached, who are only too flattered to be hit on by a fine looking woman like her."

"Hit on?" Canal echoed, feigning incomprehension of the aggressive metaphor recently adopted in American circles that had almost thoroughly supplanted idioms like flirting with, coming on to, and making a move on. He traced out a curving motion with his forearm and fist as if he were about to pound on the table and looked at her enquiringly.

Jocelyn giggled at his gestural attempt to understand and exclaimed, "You're right, there is something brutal about the expression, but all it really means is to flirt with someone."

The inspector was not as inclined as the librarian seemed to be to dismiss the import of the violence in the metaphor that had taken by storm the North American dating population in less than a decade. People had, he was sure, a number of ways of expressing more or less the same thing at their disposal, and if they all began opting for a particularly aggressive idiom, it was not necessarily just because it was the newest and hippest, or should he say raddest? Perhaps relations among people had, he reflected, truly become more punishing. Unless it simply signaled a belated return to the ancient Greek practice whereby a man would throw an apple at a woman he was interested in, and if she picked it up after it struck her, it was a sign that his love for her might be reciprocated. Somehow, he doubted that, and moreover the roles were inverted in the present case ...

But for the sake of argument, Canal was willing to set his objections aside and accept the librarian's premise that there was nothing abusive in Drago's "hitting on" men wheresoever she roamed. "So wherein lies the harm?" asked Canal, playing up his role as a supposedly liberal-minded Frenchman.

"You mean *other* than the fact that she waylays many a woman's husband?" Jocelyn replied, unwittingly reintroducing the theme of violent attacks.

The tone with which her rhetorical question was put suggested to Canal's ears that the librarian had had overly intimate experience with Drago's machinations, her ambushing having perhaps struck a little too close to home. "Yes," he concurred, "I mean other than that."

"Her emotional life remains incredibly impoverished," Jocelyn observed, with a curious admixture of concern and criticism. "Some may find it glamorous to sleep with so many different men, but I think she's actually the loneliest woman I know—and New York is full of lonely women, I can tell you that!"

Canal confined his comments to the guttural "Hmm."

"It gets old never having anyone to come home to."

"Maybe it does not bother Mademoiselle Drago."

"Oh, but it does. She's confided to me on several occasions. Why, just a few weeks ago, we were getting a bit loaded together at the bar at the annual gala ..."

Canal made a twisting motion with his fist placed on the tip of his nose as if to query whether *loaded* meant *drunk*.

His interlocutor nodded and went on, "… and she spilled her guts to me about how even a second date seemed to be becoming a scarce commodity these days."

"At the cash bar at the gala—*tiens, tiens*," the inspector said to himself. Then, addressing his thoughts to Jocelyn, he opined, "Perhaps she leaves too little to the imagination after the first date?"

"That's what I've been telling her for years," the librarian proclaimed, happy to learn that even a Frenchman might share her opinion. "I guess we could all learn a thing or two from girls like Doreen who never really give *yes* for an answer …"

As she trailed off, the purported professor looked at her quizzically.

"Oh," she explained, "I was just thinking about the foolish rumors going around about how Doreen was killed by one of the men she had been leading on."

"She had been leading someone on?" Canal asked, affecting naïveté.

"Several different someones, and each of their names has been put forward, but I say the rumormongers are all barking up the wrong tree."

"In effect?" he asked, translating directly from the French, the pertinence of the discussion dissuading him from making the librarian explain the dog-barking-at-cat-in-tree metaphor. "Why is that?"

"They're all looking in the wrong direction within the hierarchy. They're all seeking the culprit," she pursued her isocolon, "among those who had power over Doreen, whereas they should be looking in the opposite direction."

"At those over whom Doreen had power?"

"Bingo."

"Did she know things about certain people that gave her leverage over them?"

"I don't really know. But it's funny," she added, smiling wryly, "that at an institution that is ostensibly devoted to

110

alleviating at least some of the suffering of humankind, hardly anyone ever thinks of the patients!"

"The patients? You think she was killed by one of the patients?"

"Anyone with half a brain could tell that Doreen was practicing wild analysis. She seemed to me to have an uncanny knack for pressing her patients' buttons."

"Do you suspect any one of them in particular?" Kappferrant asked, wide-eyed.

"As you have no doubt noticed, the library is a bit far down the hall from the clinic. I only occasionally see patients come and go and never learn their names, but I can almost always guess which ones are Doreen's by their agitated and slightly crazed looks as they leave the clinic and stand by the elevator. One of them has even taken to dressing almost exactly like her. Another one dyes her hair a different color every week.

"The fact," she went on, "that nobody has so much as suggested one of their names shows just how caught up in the power struggles with their semblables, their supposed fellow analysts, everyone is around here. The only passions they think exist are those bubbling in the cauldron of NIPPLES's hallowed halls."

"As if they believed that the only people who could possibly take any real action are the analysts themselves," Canal chimed in.

"I may get laughed at for consulting the constellations, but they're all busy contemplating their navels!"

Jocelyn struck him thus far as a fair judge of character, especially when compared to most of those he had spoken with at the Institute. He decided to feel her out about the recent divorcee, having reflected, in the taxi back to the Institute from City University, that the anthropologist had managed to sprinkle the words *cure*, *torment*, and *momentous* into her remarks during the interview. "The police, I hear, believe

Madame Watkins was the culprit," he commented. "You lend no credence to their accusation?"

"If you told me that Wilma had murdered her ex-husband Willy, I'd believe you in a heartbeat," she replied, eyeing her interlocutor keenly. "She played her role as supportive wife admirably at all the NIPPLES social events, but always struck me as a gruff and angry woman who was infuriated at her husband for God only knew what!"

"Infuriated?"

"Yep," the librarian nodded. "You'd think I would have gotten to know her better over the years, the two of us being married to men who spent so much time together. But she's a very private person, in her own way." She shook her head slowly. "I've never been like that—when I'm incensed, everybody knows right away, especially when it's because of one of my husbands!"

"Whereas Madame Watkins ...?"

"Is all calm on the outside and boiling over on the inside."

"You do not think she wanted her husband to leave her?"

"Sure, why not?" she opined sardonically. "But she was also desperate to keep him. You know how it is with certain couples," she said, glancing at the historian's unadorned left hand. "They can't stand to be together and they can't stand to be apart."

Kappferrant nodded sadly and pensively.

"I can't imagine her going after some stranger, even if she suspected her of wanting to steal her Willy from her."

The professor was unable to suppress a laugh, which quickly led to shared hilarity.

CHAPTER NINETEEN

Saturday noon found Jean-Pierre Kappferrant entering Central Park in the direction of the Tavern on the Green. Peterson, Doreen's former analyst and one of NIPPLES's head honchos, presumably wanting to maintain the upper hand, had pre-empted the offer the analyst knew the Frenchman had been making to all and sundry at the Institute to treat them to lunch in exchange for an interview by inviting the historian to his favorite haunt—a haunt which he felt no foreigner could afford to pass up the opportunity to visit, especially as reservations were impossible to come by.

As the Frenchman strolled over to the overpriced hostelry where he expected to lunch no better than he had in the eateries located within a hundred yards of the Institute, at the favorite spots of the many trainees he had invited out, he mulled over the information he had received from NYPD Inspector Ponlevek that morning. Doreen Sheehy's police record was impeccable, whether because she had scrupulously stayed on the right side of the law or because her family had always had enough pull to ensure that whatever charges might have been levied against her during her twenty-nine summers were more or less promptly dropped.

But her friend Rosalynn Thompson had a police file as thick as Ponlevek's fist—about the size of a small ham, as Canal recalled—comprised of myriad drug charges. They ranged from possession of small amounts of dope of one kind or another—most of which had been dismissed on technicalities, like lack of proper search warrants, or worked off by community service—to dealing drugs herself. And it was not just any drugs she had been selling in her most recent charges: it was *prescription pain pills*, the very kind Doreen was addicted to, if her boyfriend Lou were to be believed. If Rosalynn had always managed to avoid serving time—something the see no evil, hear no evil NIPPLES Admissions Committee would probably never have discovered anyway—it was by dint of a stratagem on her part that seemed particularly relevant to the case at hand: she ratted on her accomplices in exchange for a suspended sentence or the dismissal of charges.

Rosalynn, having discovered Doreen's lack of the sheep-skin required for admission to the training program, might have threatened to fink on Doreen if she did not stop kissing ass so brazenly. Doreen—who might well have known about Rosalynn's criminal record, since the two trainees had supposedly been joined at the hip for three years—might have countered that she would report Rosalynn's criminal activities to the Education Committee. A desperate Rosalynn might then have played her last card by threatening to cut off Doreen's supply of pills—it stood to reason, after all, that these past few years Rosalynn had been Doreen's primary purveyor of pallia-tives for the pain of existence.

Had Doreen dared her to, confident that she could obtain her colorful little friends elsewhere and well aware that Rosalynn needed the greenbacks that Doreen had in sackfuls, Rosalynn might have opted for stronger medicine: curare slipped into the little, rounded gel capsules Doreen had grown so fond of. The inspector believed he had heard that oral administration of curare usually did not have much effect, but if Doreen had swallowed a pill on an empty stomach, there might have been a fair chance of poisoning.

A lot of "might haves," Canal reflected, but they would certainly make Rosalynn a well-situated accomplice to Wilma Watkins, assuming the latter were, despite the librarian's views, seeking revenge on the student who had lured her husband away. Two birds, the inspector mused, would obtain satisfaction with one tiny pebble, and there would have been no need whatsoever for either of the birds to be present at the convention luncheon. The pinprick on Doreen's arm might have nothing to do with her death at all—perhaps she had simply stuck herself with a safety pin while dressing that morning.

Canal recalled that he had been unable to find Rosalynn's name on the seating chart, but then that concerned the Saturday night gala anyway, not the Sunday luncheon at which the girl had collapsed.

He made a mental note to ask Ponlevek to have the lab analyze all the pills in Doreen's medicine cabinet at home, in her desk at work, and on her person at the time of death—not forgetting the wrap she had likely left in the coatroom. Rosalynn might have laced a whole batch of pills to ensure that Doreen passed on soon after the transaction, or just one pill which Doreen might have popped at any time in the next couple of weeks. A whole bottle of benzos cut with curare would constitute useful proof against the supposed best friend. And, who knew? The police might even be able to lift some fingerprints off the pills and containers.

CHAPTER TWENTY

A rriving at the infamous restaurant which, as Canal knew from the papers, was not much longer for this world than Doreen herself had been, the postiche professor was led by the maître d'hôtel to a table commanding a fine view of the park. George Peterson was sitting there with a young boy of ten or eleven who was presented to Kappferrant as Peterson's nephew Jason.

"Jason will not be joining us for lunch, appearances to the contrary notwishstanding," Peterson began pompously, without standing, even as he slurred his words slightly, "only for dessert. Off you go," he said to the boy, flicking the fingers of one hand toward him as if to chase him away like a fly.

"My sister's son," he uttered, as if by way of explanation. "Damn nuishance! Her youngest had to go in for a medical procedure, so I got stuck with the eldest—as if he couldn't read a book in the waiting room like everyone else."

The inspector noted to himself that Peterson seemed to have gotten a considerable head start on the liquid portion of the meal and was already fairly *éméché*. He wondered what kind of existential pain the analyst must be grappling with to have already downed, by twelve-thirty on a Saturday morning, what appeared to have been three martinis, if one could judge from the empty glasses strewn across the table and the supposition that he had not shared them with his uncherished nephew.

Hearing Peterson call over the head waiter, with whom he was evidently on a first name basis, and order a hefty repast for the two of them, complete with a full bottle of Italian wine—without so much as a "by your leave" uttered in the professor's general direction—the inspector calculated that several things would become clear in fairly short order. It appeared that Peterson intended to direct the proceedings, and that Canal need but sit back and go along for the ride, however bumpy it might be. He turned on his recording device and set out a pad and Montblanc fountain pen.

Like everyone else at the Institute, Peterson had by now heard plenty in the wings, coffee cubby, and on the couch about the kinds of questions the historian was asking. He proceeded to provide the Frenchman with his own vainglorious version of the progress of Calanianism. It not surprisingly featured his own work prominently, and he promulgated the importance of his contributions shamelessly.

"I've been saying for years that analysts must not cause their patients any dishcomfort or distress whatsoever, no matter what the personal cost to themselves," he proffered in a heroic strain. "Clinicians who ask all kinds of indiscreet questions provoke anxiety in their clients, which doesn't help the latter a whit—it's the exact opposite of what practitioners should be screwing," he concluded emphatically. "I mean doing."

"So you think that every topic can be addressed in ze course of therapy without generating any discomfort on the patient's part?"

"Naturally," Peterson replied. "You just have to wait until the patient is ready and brings the topic up himself."

"What if he never does?"

"*Never* is a strong word—we must be prepared to wait for years if need be."

"And what if even after years, the patient never brings up certain topics? Must not the analyst do something to elicit the material that is being left out?"

"Patients like that are unanalyzable! I've been saying this for decades, but nobody seems to listen ...," he trailed off and swilled half a glass of red wine in one gulp. "Haven't you tread my paper from nineteen eighty-four on unanalyzability?"

"I have, but I confess it made me think that, from your point of view, virtually everyone is unanalyzable." The inspector did not want to openly attack Peterson's perspective, yet he could not help but add, "I do not believe I have ever heard of a single successful case in which the analysand spontaneously spoke about everything that needed to be explored, in which the analyst did not have to work hard to draw out material related to embarrassing and, indeed, traumatic subjects."

"That's just because everyone is so damned impatient these days. If you give the client enough time, he'll come out with these things himself."

"Without any distress or anxiety?"

"Oh," Peterson replied, quaffing another half-glass of wine and garbling his words anew, "he may experience some discomfort, but *we* won't be the ones who have indouched it."

"Is that so very important? Not to be seen as someone who asks difficult, probing questions?"

"Our first duty is to do no harm," he replied, blithely citing Hippocrates.

"What about doing some good?"

"We do good by doing no harm," the analyst replied platitudinously. "Neutrality is our most sacred virtue."

"What exactly do you mean by neutrality?" Kappferrant asked, pen at the ready to transcribe the eminent analyst's views.

"Every topic the patient discusses is treated with equal interest."

"Even if the patient recites the phone book to you, or every film he has ever watched? Even if he is clearly prevaricating?"

"We have to wait him out."

"Does that not take an inordinately long time?"

"Analysis is a lifetime endeavor," the analyst replied, looking fondly at the red wine he had just poured himself, for he was consuming the juice far too quickly for the otherwise attentive wait staff to keep his glass full. He gestured to the head waiter to bring a second bottle of the same. "We only require four years of analysis for the purposes of training at American institutes, but I always thrive to hold on to the trainees for four or five times as long."

The professor feigned intense interest by jotting down a few notes on the pad, above all his interlocutor's ever lengthening list of slips and slurs, and the analyst went on.

"You can't get a whole sheck of a lot done in four hort years—for example, with this one patient of mine, we have spent ...," he interrupted himself, and began anew, "we spent almost three full years talking about just two dreams. Pretty amazing, huh?" he added, eyeing the historian keenly.

Canal was rather more concerned than impressed. He cocked an eyebrow and enquired, "Just two dreams? They must have been incredibly long and multifaceted!"

"No," the other shook his head. Realizing that the sommelier had confused this gesture with a rejection of the newly arrived bottle, he instructed the attendant to open and serve, and then resumed his denial. "They were quite ordinary dreams, as a fatter of mact, I mean of tact. Well, you know what I mean ... The first involved the patient's family home being on fire and her mother wanting to run upstairs to retrieve her jewelry box. The second depicted the patient receiving a letter that her father was dead and learning when she finally got home that everyone was already at the semenary—I mean cemetery."

Canal was stunned for some moments and could not respond.

He finally reassembled his wits and gingerly asked the venerable training analyst whether or not either of those dreams had sounded familiar to him in any way, shape, or form when they were told to him by his analysand. Peterson made it plain he had no idea what the good professor was talking about. The fact that a hundred years earlier, Freud's famous patient, who went down in history under the name Dora, had told Freud those same two dreams, and that they had been the centerpiece of his controversial presentation of her three-month stint of therapy with him, would apparently be news to Peterson.

Kappferrant did not take it upon himself to convey such news then and there, sensing that the analyst was already too sodden to absorb it. The inspector had no doubt but that the trainee in question was Doreen—why else would Peterson have corrected his verb tense from the imperfect to the perfect? She showed signs of having had a sense of humor in choosing her virtually eponymous predecessor as a model for her own thoroughly bogus analysis—as Lou had conjectured, Doreen had probably made up at least half of what she told her shrink—allowing her to make a mockery of Peterson's knowledge of psychoanalysis at the same time. Or, alternatively, perhaps she had genuinely come to confuse herself with Freud's infamous analysand …

"My work with this woman was fascinating, fooly tracinating," the analyst exclaimed, all the while seemingly oblivious to his interlocutor's change of countenance. Canal wondered if the excessively harmless doctor believed it was also illicit to ask his patients about a sudden smile or frown, a laugh, smirk, or lapsing into silence. On the other hand, maybe he simply did not notice such things, considering how little attention he seemed to be paying to them even in a social situation such as this. The inspector was convinced the American would never dare be so intrusive as to ask patients what was going through their minds! Granted, he conceded to himself, whatever powers

121

of perception the practitioner had under normal circumstances were seriously compromised at present.

"But it's all come to naught now," Peterson blubbered, as if he were about to burst into tears. He rose with some difficulty and stumbled in the general direction of the restroom without even excusing himself.

CHAPTER TWENTY-ONE

Jean-Pierre Kappferrant poured himself what little wine Peterson had not already tossed down the hatch, thereby "unintentionally" necessitating abstemious behavior on the part of his guest. He reflected that Caroline Drago had characterized the training analyst as besotted with his young, attractive patient, and that Peterson was duly showing signs of missing watching her wriggle on the couch before him. Could that be the secret source of pain in his existence?

Or was he merely expressing regret at something he himself had done, after hearing from Watkins that for years Doreen had been pulling the wool over his eyes regarding her approach to practice, a regret that required considerable quantities of alcohol to quell?

Canal's musings were interrupted by the return of Jason who had come to collect on his uncle's promise of just desserts for having let them break bread in peace.

He seated himself horseback style on the chair without the slightest ceremony and asked, "You have a funny accent, mister. Where you from?"

"I am from France," Canal replied. "Have you ever been there?"

"Uh uh," he responded, shaking his head. "My mother went there, though, when she was still married to my father—we had to stay with Uncle George."

"Not much fun, *hein*?" Canal sympathized.

"You can say that again," the boy responded wryly. "You have poisons over there too?"

The inspector was slightly taken aback.

As he remained for some moments unsure how to respond, the boy continued, "You know, like that rhododendron stuff everybody's been talking about lately. I've got some that I use on the butterflies, frogs, and snakes I catch whenever we go out to Grandpa's house in the Catskills. I love watching them get all bug-eyed when I stick 'em with it," he gushed.

"Your mother lets you play with poison?" Canal was incredulous.

"Yeah," he replied unconcernedly. "At first she didn't like it when Uncle George gave me some pins dipped in it, but he showed me how to use it right."

"Any idea where he gets it from?" Canal asked as if casually.

"From some friend of his, I think—actually a friend's wife, some kind of architect or archaeologist or something like that."

"You wouldn't happen to recall her—"

Peterson staggered back to the table looking a bit green about the gills and the inspector's tête-à-tête with Jason was cut short.

CHAPTER TWENTY-TWO

Canal adjusted his belt in front of the mirror that evening and reflected that Ferguson had done a pretty outstanding job finding a wearable costume at such short notice. As he dressed, he meditated upon his talk with Peterson and found it hard to believe that such a brainless wreck of a man could intellectually or politically dominate anyone.

The tippler's approach to technique obviously turned analysis into a kind of Chinese water torture for analysts. Their hands were tied by the theory of practice itself: they were not allowed to arouse any anxiety whatsoever, even though discomfort is often necessary for patients to overcome inhibitions, embarrassment, and other barriers to speech. Nor were they permitted to solicit associations to slips, fantasies, or dreams—why, if Peterson had his way, analysts would have to view whatever else the patient says in a session as possible associations to them, no matter how unrelated.

"Imagine making a career out of teaching analysts to play dead," he exclaimed to himself. "I myself would make a terrible neo-Calanian, curious and prying as I am. I could never wait years for someone to begin to tell me her deepest wishes and fantasies. On the plus side," he ruminated, "rather more of the population would prove to be analyzable. Never prying or insinuating that slips, slurs, or double entendres might mean more than they think—well, that might make perfect sense in working with psychotics, but hardly with neurotics. Again the error," the inspector mused, "of treating one diagnostic group just like the other, as if clinicians could not tell the difference between them. Thankfully, at least some criminologists can …"

Canal laughed at his reflection in the mirror as he tried to picture what his own face must have looked like when Peterson told him about the three-year analysis that had focused on but two borrowed dreams. His jaw must have dropped about a mile and his eyes must have shown every sign of *sidération*: astonishment and shock must have been written all over his face.

At the end of their meeting Kappferrant had casually advised Peterson to *re*read Freud's *Fragment of a Case of Hysteria*. In doing so, the Frenchman had disingenuously taken it for granted that, at some point in the course of the American's training, he had no doubt read at least a few pages of Freud's work. But the inspector knew full well that, back when Peterson had been a trainee, it was already fashionable in the US to read nothing but authors who wrote in English. The wholesale forgetting of Freud had become nearly unstoppable since then …

Adjusting his fake horseshoe-shaped mustache so that it would be even in the mirror, the thought occurred to him that at least someone at the Institute must be reading Freud, for Doreen obviously had—though probably before she matriculated … He wondered, suddenly, if Doreen had not in fact mimicked Dora in other ways, symbolically slapping Watkins and Peterson like Dora had slapped Herr K., or giving Peterson two weeks' notice like a simple employee as Dora had done with Freud, with the possible twist that Doreen intended to leave Peterson differently than Dora had left Freud. Dora, after all, had at least made a show of attempting to resume her analysis with Freud some fifteen months later, but Freud, having been too disappointed by his own inability to help her and indeed handle her, had been unwilling to take up the work anew ...

A thought that had never occurred to Canal in the three weeks since Ponlevek first came to talk with him about the case suddenly flashed through his mind: perhaps rumors of her being murdered had been greatly exaggerated. Perhaps the curare had been self-administered!

The inspector sank down on a chair in his dressing room. "Did that make any sense?" he asked himself, his thoughts awhirl. "Could that possibly make any sense?" Had Doreen been testing her analyst, hoping against hope that he would see through her lies and ruses and finally bring her to say something in her own name, something about her own anguish, wishes, and joys?

Had she really been as cynically calculating as certain of her colleagues made her out to be? Granted, she had—Ponlevek had double checked this—entered the NIPPLES training program under false pretenses, asserting that she had completed her Psy.D. when she had been dismissed from her program at that university Canal could never quite remember the name of. What was it called, Unfarely Sonofarichard U.?

But perhaps she had still had a glimmer of faith in psychoanalysis upon entering the program, believing in some small corner of her mind that it could help her handle the pain of existence better than the pills she had been taking. One need not necessarily chalk up her pill popping to cynicism—one could alternatively view it simply as a product of this age of medication. Virtually everyone around her was as medicated as she was, taking one kind of pill to make them alert or aroused, another to make them relax, one to wake them up in the morning, and another to put them to sleep at night. For it was also the age of sleeplessness, Canal mused, most people's daily life activities being detached from any kind of natural cycle like the waxing and waning of daylight, their nights extending indefinitely in front of a flickering or blinking screen … Maybe something in Sheehy had wanted to get rid of all those pills.

"What a funny surname she had!" the inspector reflected, not for the first time. He was sure that Peterson never broached the hermaphroditism inherent in her last name and that the girl's sexuality remained a closed book to both George and herself. It was, after all, against the man's religion to ask about sexual fantasies patients might have other than the so-called plain vanilla ones they spontaneously told him, assuming they told him any at all.

If only Doreen had been assigned an analyst who could have recognized and worked around the deceptions endemic to hysteria, the dissimulations and fabrications she could not prevent herself from producing in such profusion … Maybe she realized she could not help herself, these things just coming over her and coming out of her, but hoped that someone else might be able to help her—help her stop imitating, simulating, fabricating, and omitting.

A woman like Caroline Drago would have obviously been a better choice for an inveterate liar like Doreen. The girl would probably have been less inclined to play the same seductive games with a woman than with a man, and the seasoned dragon lady did not strike Canal as the kind to fall for a pile of … he completed the sentence with "phony-baloney" so as not to have to excuse his own French to himself. In any case, a female analyst might sooner have taken umbrage at Doreen's beauty and seductive manner than be charmed by them and might have been considerably more likely to recognize Doreen's ploys and decoys for what they were.

A pity Drago had never been allowed to become a training analyst and thus had never even been in the running to become Doreen's analyst. This whole line of thought was pointless, Canal suddenly reflected, realizing that if the Admissions Committee had been perceptive enough to assign Doreen to

Caroline Drago, they would ineluctably have divined enough about her to never have accepted her in the first place!

Returning to his earlier train of thought, Canal mused that if Doreen had still had a shred of faith in psychoanalysis prior to entering the program, her training analyst's approach would surely have eradicated it. He refused to ask her anything that might upset her, he was blind to her obvious plagiarism of Ida Bauer, a.k.a. Dora, and he seemed willing to believe she harbored no envy, anger, or resentment toward him or anyone else! All those failings, when demonstrated and reconfirmed five times a week for three years, would have been enough to dash anyone's hopes ...

Rising from the armchair to finish dressing, Canal concluded that suicide could not be completely ruled out, especially since it had been committed right under Peterson's nose. An incorrigible brown-noser like Doreen had almost certainly sat with the same powerbrokers at the Sunday midday meal as she had at the gala the night before, he reflected, even though Ponlevek had confirmed that there were no assigned seats for the awards luncheon. Her possible *passage à l'acte* would thus have occurred at a table Doreen shared with all the Institute's bigwigs at the most important Calanian convention of the year. If that was not sending a message of despair to her analyst and to her school, Canal did not know what could count as one!

Had Doreen perhaps wanted to inscribe a Dantean message to every other potential trainee and analysand on the Institute's front door—"Abandon hope all ye who enter here"?

Adding the final accouterments, Canal placed the black cowboy hat on his head. "How would Clint Eastwood have worn it?" he asked himself, as he tilted it at various angles. "Not much of a gunslinger," he observed to himself as he surveyed his bearing in the full-length mirror. Bowing his legs, he imagined himself on horseback and tried to stand the way he had seen sheriffs and hired guns stand in shootouts at high noon in many a Western, hands poised just inches above his six-shooters.

"Not much of a killer," he said to himself, concluding his visual examination of the other with the star on his chest in the mirror. Then again, Peterson had not struck him as much of a killer either, but one never knew how severely the training analyst's precious im(a)ge of himself had been threatened by Watkins's revelations to him at the gala dinner. If Peterson had had a murderous bone in his body, there was no sign of it now—only of its flip side, regret—but it was not altogether impossible that he was craftier than he let on. Did Aristotle not say to always prefer the probable impossible to the improbable possible, whatever that meant? And had Peterson not maneuvered his way to the top of NIPPLES? His drunken blubbering might be a show he was putting on, all the better to disguise ceaseless premeditated activity, like that of the universal spider, Louis XI, or of Poe's Minister D—. Peterson might merely be playing possum ... Well, if it was not exactly possum, it was some sort of *poudre aux yeux* all the same, he mused, some sort of dissimulation.

"*Plus ça va, plus ça s'embrouille*," Canal exclaimed to himself. Each new person he interviewed in this case seemed to have a definite reason for seeking revenge on Doreen, and there seemed to be far too much of this rare poison in circulation around her. Either there was a thread he was missing that somehow connected all of these potential actors, he reflected, or he was overlooking some crucial fact. Well, actually it was not an either/or: one never knew how much of the story one was missing at any point in time until later.

CHAPTER TWENTY-THREE

There were so many people in attendance at Caroline Drago's costume party and so many disguised beyond recognition that for the first five minutes Canal almost wondered if he had come to the right address. Finely carved Halloween jack-o'-lanterns graced the entrance to her posh penthouse suite and the interior was decorated in sophisticated black and orange tones. Balloons and lights had not been stuck here and there willy-nilly as at many homespun parties. The hostess had done the place up right, and had hired a bartender and a three-piece rock band which belted out "The Monster Mash," "Thriller," and "Ghostbusters" in rapid succession upon Canal's arrival.

Luckily, the inspector's disguise was not so complete as to prevent an elegantly but scantily clad Cleopatra, a.k.a. Drago, from spotting him. She immediately came over and greeted him warmly and effusively. She was carrying a golden goblet of ambrosia and offered it to him.

Then, attaching herself to his arm, she directed the sheriff hither and thither, pointing out various people whose disguises she had managed to see through whom he might know from the Institute, but also from the music and art worlds as well.

Canal cringed upon hearing her mention that people from the New York music scene were present, because a number of them knew him as Quesjac Canal. But he consoled himself with the thought that Drago probably did not travel in the same circles as his friend Rolland Saalem, the well-known conductor of the New York Philharmonic Orchestra. If it turned out that she did, Canal would do his best to bring the maestro abreast of the situation as quickly and discreetly as possible.

A number of the Institute top brass were in attendance. William Watkins, affecting ancient sagacity, was garbed in a Roman toga, a laurel crown capping his daunting dome and sandals adorning his swollen feet. George Peterson, going for a rather different effect, was dressed as Satan, complete with a five-foot fork and a long pointed tail. The inspector noted that, although Uncle George looked a tad peaked around the edges after his excesses earlier that day, he was not confining his consumption to tomato juice, preferring a little of the hair of the dog that had bitten him. "A pretty bizarre expression," Canal mused to himself, searching his memory banks for some sort of equivalent in French, to no avail. Whether, despite this linguistic lacuna, Gauls engaged in a similar strategy to overcome hangovers, he could not be sure. In any case, Peterson did not seem terribly the worse for wear, suggesting that what had appeared to Canal to be a lunchtime exploit was perhaps something more along the lines of an everyday occurrence in the analyst's life.

Despite being from the dreaded, much ostracized and demonized middle group, Drago had invited analysts and trainees young and old from all the NIPPLES factions and even from other psychoanalytic societies as well. Canal was able to pick out quite a few of the trainees he had met, although many revelers were so heavily or cleverly costumed that he could not fathom their true identities. It occurred to him that he did not see one of them, the girl whose coffee he had spilled his very first day at NIPPLES, and that he had not since then run into her again, in any sense of the expression. Perhaps she had been ill … Or had decorating her new office been taking up all of her time?

An image from a dream he had had the night before suddenly flashed through his mind, but it was difficult to bring it into focus given the commotion surrounding him: a young, elegantly attired brunette wearing a string of pearls …

His ruminations were interrupted when his hostess pointed out Rosalynn Thompson to him, sporting a Janus-faced mask, one side of which was smiling reassuringly while the other side was in the throes of fury. The inspector was bowled over by the concordance between her choice of costume and his speculations about her.

The next acquaintance of his that Drago spotted was Jocelyn Josephs, the librarian, who was dancing on the opposite side of the spacious room. She was letting out her inner Barbara Eden, dressed in a revealing genie outfit marrying pink and purple hues, and billowing myriad see-through silk scarves around her.

Canal wondered whether the female portion of the former Watkins couple was present and surveyed the crowd for spiky grayish-white hair and earrings by the dozen. But he refrained from asking his hostess if she were there, and if so who she might be dressed up as, since he did not know whether they had been on friendly terms, or whether Caroline would have invited Wilma Watkins to such a NIPPLES-heavy event even if they had been, given the circumstances.

New arrivals soon forced Drago to abandon her armrest, although she assured Kappferrant that she would be back soon—as much a promise as a threat given the way she expressed it—and the sheriff wended his way among the crowd toward Henry Bowman, the NIPPLES clinic secretary, whom he had noticed leaning against the bar and watching the tight mass of costumed dancers writhing around the living room floor.

Henry was fitted out in a Sherlock Holmes get-up, complete with the infamous sleuth's pipe and ever-so-British hat. He was looking rather morose, but his face brightened upon recognizing the gunslinger at several paces and he greeted Kappferrant enthusiastically. "How goes your research, my dear Watson," he quipped, thinking this terribly droll.

"*Pas trop mal*," the professor replied to the erstwhile French speaker, "but I have to admit to having gotten somewhat side-tracked, given all this talk about the death at the Institute."

"Indeed," Henry nodded gravely, stroking his chin and affecting to smoke his unlit pipe. "The rumors about what happened have intensified in the past week."

"Since you are wearing your detective's hat, would you mind helping me with a few questions that have been on my mind?"

"Assuming they are elementary, my dear Watson," the other replied, happy to chat with the quirky Parisian again. "But the music is too loud here to talk—let us retire to a quieter location." Canal agreed with a simple head sign, and Henry went on, "But first, what are you drinking?"

Canal requested champagne and Henry ordered and received two overflowing glasses from the barman before they set off, not into the sunset, but out onto the penthouse terrace. It was far from dark, owing to the myriad lights of the New York skyline, and there were small garden lights lining the path out to the deck. Luckily for them, it was one of those years when, instead of bringing bone-chilling temperatures at Halloween, the weather was quite balmy.

"You are familiar with all of the patients at the NIPPLES clinic, are you not?" Canal began as they leaned against the rail, gazing out over the city that never sleeps.

"Oh yes," Henry replied, "they all check in with me at the window when they arrive so that I can alert their analysts that they are there."

"Do you see them again when they leave?"

"Ah, you put your finger there on a delicate subject. They are all supposed to come by to pay their bill and to schedule their next appointment, but some have no money, some refuse to pay, some are so upset they can't bear to look at me much less talk for thirty seconds, and some are so infuriated they storm out without paying or scheduling their next appointment."

"Were Doreen's patients any different than other people's in that regard?"

"They were, now that you mention it," the sleuth for a day replied. "I don't know if they were just an ornery bunch or whether she made them that way, but they did a lot more storming out than anyone else's. I was constantly calling them to set appointment times, and getting money from them was like prizing honey from a bear! I never really thought about it before, but her patients in particular were almost always unwilling to pay." A chorus of car horns wafted up from the street far below them.

"Interesting," the self-appointed historian said, stroking his mustache. "*Alors*, my dear Herlock Sholmes, you are a perceptive man and I am sure you have your own view of the matter—what do you make of all that?"

"I suspect she was a pretty awful therapist."

"Uh huh," Canal mused, inadvertently making a sound that would have immediately tipped Henry off that Kappferrant was not who he professed to be, had Henry been more attuned to the paralinguistic sounds made by Americans that are never made by the French. "And did you get the impression that she treated certain patients better than others, or that she was particularly awful with some of them?"

The young man contemplated this. "Come to think of it," he answered slowly, "there was one guy who almost always came late, but she always gave him a full forty-five minutes and often even kept him an extra half-hour."

"Why do you think that was?"

"I think she just liked talking with him," Henry said, smiling derisively. "They'd get talking about something and she'd lose track of time. It got so bad sometimes that her next patient was kept waiting forever and got—"

"A variable-length session?" the gunman cut in slyly.

"Shortchanged, I'd say," Henry riposted. "Doreen would get back on schedule with whoever was next, sometimes giving 'em only fifteen or twenty minutes so she would have time to run to the bathroom or get a cup of coffee."

"Wasn't the next patient almost always the same person?"

"Fortunately not, but it did happen pretty regularly to the same two or three people."

"What was this favored patient's name?"

"Derek, Derek Cepe, if I'm not mistaken," proffered the sleuth, after a siren from the avenue below had stopped its plaintive wail.

Canal made a mental note of this. "Do you recall there being any one patient who seemed to get particularly irate about Doreen's methods?" he resumed his questioning.

"Yeah, Sue Spechtor, one of the ones frequently treated to short sessions. She did a lot of yelling and knocked over lamps and chairs."

"Any idea what that was about?" Canal asked, his eyes narrowing.

Henry, who was enjoying this bit of Holmesian banter, replied, "I'm afraid not, my dear Watson. What goes on behind closed doors ..."

"Yes, hard to know," the professor sympathized, the patient's name alone sufficing to incline Canal to add her to his list of potential poisoners. Affecting to continue the S & H game, he enquired, "Did you ever get the sense that Doreen socialized with or got involved with any of her patients?"

"You mean romantically?"

"For example."

"Not that I know of. But you never knew with her," Henry added acerbically, letting his guard down. "How did you wind up taking your investigation in this direction? You suspect there's something about neo-Calanianism that brings out the worst in people and makes them do desperate things?"

"Good thinking!" Canal thought to himself. "This Sherlock is truly working for me." Then, aloud, he uttered, "*Je ne vous le fais pas dire!*"

Henry was unfamiliar with the idiomatic meaning of the interjection and took it literally. "You mean, you ...," he trailed off, seeming not to dare complete the thought.

Canal diplomatically backpedaled a little. "Every school of analysis has its malcontents, do not misconstrue my meaning. Suicide and aggressive acts do occasionally occur no matter what the theoretical approach taken."

Henry seemed slightly relieved. "Unlike yourself," he began, "I've never studied the history of psychoanalysis or looked in any detail at the problems encountered at other schools."

"It never hurts to study the history of your field," the self-styled professor asserted. "It can help you avoid repeating mistakes made in the past, and avoid thinking that some new idea that popped into your mind will ameliorate things when many a time and oft' it has already proved useless." Kappferrant turned away from the skyline and sat on the rail facing the penthouse. "Naturally, Doreen's problems may have had nothing whatsoever to do with neo-Calanianism. She may not have been following Calanian technique in the slightest— indeed, from what I have heard, she was just making it up as she went along."

"So I may simply have been helping her get away with breaking every rule in the book?"

"The things we do for love," Canal observed, alluding to their conversation two weeks earlier, and putting a name on the *she* that Henry had inadvertently let out of the bag at the restaurant bar that day.

"I'm not so sure it was for love, in the end," Henry expostulated, looking down at his feet, not even aware that Canal had had to put two and two together to come to this conclusion, since he had been unable to recall what he had told the professor at the restaurant that evening. "I wanted her badly, I admit it. But I was lucid enough to realize she didn't love me. She courted everyone with power at the Institute and the more redoubtable a player he was, the more assiduously she courted him. But I didn't care—I just wanted her to let me have my way with her, whether she loved me or not."

Canal listened, letting the young man get it off his chest. He seemed to have interpreted Canal's "the things we do for love" as "the things we do to win love" from someone else, a gloss the inspector himself had not put on the phrase but a legitimate reading nonetheless. Either that or Henry believed he would only truly love Doreen if she loved him in return, or if he at least cared whether she loved him back …

The music blaring from the penthouse redoubled in intensity now and the young man turned around and sat on the rail, looking toward the spinning dancers in the living room. "I guess I hoped she would feel I was such a good lover that she wouldn't be able to get enough of me, and that she would sooner or later have to fall in love with me."

"Do women operate that way? Has a woman ever gone wild for your lovemaking and then fallen in love with you? I do not believe I have ever heard of any such thing."

"I can't say I have either," the sometime sleuth admitted, looking down, "but you can't stop a guy from hoping, trying …" He looked up suddenly and added, "I've been so obsessed with Doreen that I think I'm starting to go nuts—I was absolutely sure I saw her coming out of the elevator in the lobby the other morning when I was heading into work at the Institute. I even ran after her, but I lost sight of her among the crowds of people out in the street. I know it's ridiculous—but I guess I keep hoping she isn't really dead."

"Were she to come back, perhaps you would not feel so guilty for having wanted her to get her comeuppance?"

Henry eyed Kappferrant narrowly. "Freud really was right sometimes," he opined. "It's amazing how guilty one can feel for merely having wished someone else harm."

"Amazing, indeed," the lawman concurred. Something crossed his mind now, although he would have been hard pressed to say why. "Do you know the cute new brunette trainee I bumped into at the clinic a couple of weeks ago?"

Holmes made no response, apparently lost in thoughts of guilt, if indeed they were not guilty thoughts.

"The one who had just been assigned a new office and was measuring it for drapes."

The boy shook his head.

"She must be a freshman, just being assigned her first patients," Canal tried to jog his memory.

Henry professed he knew of no cute brunettes in the freshman class, so Canal raised a question he had been meaning to ask Henry for some time, one he always kept up his sleeve for the lovelorn. "What struck you as so desirable about Doreen in the first place?" he asked. "Are there not, as I think you say, fish in the other sea?"

"Of course there are," Henry replied, chuckling at the professor's erroneous word order, "but, for whatever reason, I only go for the ones who aren't really interested in me and whom I can get some paltry leverage over."

"For *what* reason?" Canal asked, picking up on the young man's use of the ever-so-popular glib expression that almost invariably served to shelve the core issue.

"If only I knew … Already in high school and college I'd try to get girls to like me by helping them with their homework. Later I tried to make them feel beholden to me by buying them groceries or even paying their rent." The young man's face was almost as red as his hair now.

"Why would you want a girl to feel beholden to you? What could that possibly do for you?"

"Damned if I know!" Henry exploded. "Five years of analysis and I've never even asked myself the question."

"You must be in therapy with Peterson," Canal joked offhandedly.

"I am, as a matter of fact," Henry replied, surprised at the Frenchman's intuition.

"It might be worth investigating the question, even if it is not so elementary, my dear Sherlock," Canal bantered, a bit surprised that he had guessed correctly. "And you might want to think about changing analysts," he added, privately wondering if the fact that Doreen and Henry had been in analysis with the same man might have anything to do with Henry's fixation on her.

Henry appeared to slip into a pensive, brooding sort of mood, and Canal promised to come back out and talk with him again later in the evening. "But in the meantime," he said, "I owe it to our hostess to make an appearance on the dance floor."

CHAPTER TWENTY-FOUR

"*La fête bat son plein,*" the inspector remarked to himself upon re-entering the living room. There were even more wildly attired people than before and most of them seemed to be gyrating madly on the parquet. Picking his way with difficulty through the dense crowd, Canal located Jocelyn and attempted to dance for a few minutes in her general vicinity and in that of her current husband, the NIPPLES Society director, Harvey Josephs, whom Canal had interviewed earlier that week and who was disguised almost beyond recognition as Louis XIV. This majesty, which did not dazzle, Valéry's observation notwithstanding, struck the inspector as a particularly apt impersonation. One of the trainees had told him that Josephs was so megalomaniacal that he once bragged to his class that he had thought up but then abandoned a theory because it was too dangerous—it could predict the moment of its own emergence and that of every other theory and even the end of all theories!

Despite the comic effect of the costume selected by this perfect obsessive, Canal found Josephs to be far less entertaining company than his wife, both on the dance floor and off. Suddenly Canal's arm was grabbed from behind and he was spun around to face the Queen of the Nile, who insisted that "The Purple People Eater" was *their* song.

After writhing and grinding with his hostess to a song no Frenchman in his right mind would admit to knowing, much less one professing to be a recent arrival on North American shores, Drago affirmed no less forcefully that "Black Magic Woman" was *their* song and ensured that the professor abandoned the dance floor at no moment throughout the band's second set.

The temperature in the penthouse rose precipitously, the driving rhythms and accumulating body heat steaming up the windows. The dancers' thirst grew ever greater, and their craving could be quenched only with the heady potations proposed in profusion by the barman, who sent dancers back into the fray with round after round. The noise grew ever louder, the frenzied company singing each word of the songs along with the band, and the swirling and twirling grew faster with the relentless hammering of the bass and the palpable libidinal mojo of the crowd.

The exhilaration was collective and the inspector himself was almost dizzy when a decorated general nearby suddenly sank to the floor. It was no pratfall by the officer in fancy military dress, complete with ribbons, medals, and fake scars galore. He had been riotously laughing just moments before, while doing some rather undignified dancing to "The Time Warp" with a masked whirling dervish who was bedecked in a flowing bright red robe with a black belt, crowned with a tall tan cylindrical hat. The general was apparently overcome with heat, drink, and an intoxicating partner less than half his age ... Without missing a beat, a few NIPPLES trainees, some masquerading as Hell's Angels and others as the fratricidally inclined übershrinks Niles and Frasier Crane, lifted him off the dance floor and onto a nearby couch. There he disappeared from view behind a sea of shimmying, sequined go-go girls, sailors in uniform, Count Draculas, Frankensteins, and pirates with peg legs and parrots. The hurly-burly roared on.

It was only some ten minutes later, when the band took a break after their second set, that anyone noticed that the general had not moved a muscle since being placed on the settee.

Wilkins, one of the old school analysts who had trained in medicine prior to undergoing psychoanalytic training and had been rather more measured in his alcohol intake that evening than the twenty-odd other physicians present, shushed the crowd and examined the fallen soldier. After feeling his pulse at his wrist and neck and placing his ear next to the man's mouth and nose, he regretfully turned to Drago and pronounced him dead, adding that it was undoubtedly heart failure that had brought down the sexagenarian. The Queen of the Nile, unable to live up to her Halloween persona, shrieked, and when Canal tried to comfort her, blubbered something about her lovely party degenerating into a fiasco *à la* Mary Tyler Moore.

Ignoring references to things he should not know anything about, given his own persona, the inspector tried to console her by saying that the man had been enjoying himself considerably just moments before falling and was *mort de rire*—he quite literally died laughing. This did make her smile momentarily, but the arrival some minutes later of the ambulance crew and the defection of her guests, who began slipping out in a fairly steady stream, sent her into a funk. Although celebrating a holiday that made light of death, the revelers were neither merry nor taking the presence of a real cadaver in stride.

Canal retrieved Henry from the penthouse terrace and learned from him that the disgraced general was a standoffish neo-Calanian by the name of Sam Sorrel. He practiced out of his own home, was not a training analyst, and rarely participated in NIPPLES events, meetings, or administration. They took leave of their hostess as graciously as they could under the circumstances and left together.

CHAPTER TWENTY-FIVE

"You're a private dick?" Henry asked incredulously when—after protesting against the abduction he was being subjected to by the Frenchman who was heading south in his car, instead of north where the young man lived—Canal threw down the mask, revealing himself to be working with the NYPD on the case of Doreen's murder. "I don't believe it."

To convince him, Canal opened the left side of his vest a few inches to give the secretary a glimpse of his revolver.

"You don't think *I* did it, do you?" Henry cried. "I'd never do anything like that!"

"I admit that at first I wondered if you had had a sudden shock of some kind—learning, for example, at the NIPPLES gala that Doreen had a long-term boyfriend and that you were thus never likely to get what you had been expecting from her. But—"

"I had found out about her boyfriend a few weeks earlier," Henry explained to forestall inculpation. "I was the one who opened the convention registration forms and reply cards for the ball."

"I suspected as much. In any case, you strike me as a disappointed and bitter unrequited lover, not a killer."

"Then where are you taking me?"

"To the Institute—I want you to let me in and give me the addresses of all of Doreen's patients, especially that of Sue Spechtor."

"Sue Spechtor? Why?"

"You said she yelled, knocked over furniture, and refused to pay her bill—we are going to find out just how angry at Doreen she was."

"You suspect *her*? A woman?"

"It hadn't really occurred to me until tonight," Canal commented, pressing his foot on the accelerator after being stuck at a red light for some time, the ridiculous song "A Boy Named Sue" suddenly popping into his head. "That analyst who died at the party—had you heard anything about him being in ill health?"

"No, why do you ask?" Henry's thoughts were whirling about at a hundred miles an hour.

"I never met him before tonight, but he seemed to be dancing pretty energetically since the moment I arrived at the party, and barely looked like he had broken a sweat, whereas other people were clearly suffering from the heat and looked like they were about to pass out," the inspector observed. "There were a few older men there tonight who I would have suspected of having a heart condition, but not him—I would have sooner guessed *he* was a long-distance runner."

"You mean you think …?"

"It's merely a hunch, but just before he collapsed, he had been dancing very closely with a young woman dressed as a whirling dervish."

"And?" Henry asked, since Canal paused while he was changing lanes.

"And she was nowhere in sight when he was declared dead. In fact, now that I think of it, I don't recall seeing her at the party until shortly before that *Rocky Horror Picture Show* song was played."

146

"You mean she …?" the young man faltered again.

"I mean she might have come to the party with a very clear purpose in mind, and cleared out as soon as the deed was done."

"Dude," exclaimed the American. "Serious accusation!"

"I'm not accusing anyone of anything, not yet," the Frenchman clarified. "We are just going to have a little late-night chat with this specter and see what we can divine."

"You think anyone is going to chat with us tonight? It must be the witching hour already. Don't we need a warrant of some kind—even just to take patient records from the clinic?"

Canal glared at the young man menacingly for an instant and he immediately agreed to get with Canal's program. "There may not be any time to lose. Indeed, we may have been pussyfooting around too long already."

Henry cogitated silently for some moments. "I'm lost," he confessed. "You see some kind of connection between Doreen and Sorrel?"

Canal turned to him and avouched, "I was going to ask you the same question."

CHAPTER TWENTY-SIX

The two men pulled up in front of Sue Spechtor's building some twenty minutes later. A couple of Halloween revelers in costume exited the building just as they were about to ring her bell and they were able to enter and climb the stairs to the five-story walkup, listening to loud rock on the lower floors, but more classical yelling and screaming as they approached the fifth floor. Objects appeared to be breaking and a man and a woman seemed to be screeching at each other at the top of their lungs as Henry and Canal approached Spechtor's door.

"Follow my lead," Canal advised Henry. He knocked on the door loudly with a firm fist. "Open up! Police," he shouted.

Silence suddenly reigned within.

"Let's go! We know you're in there," Canal yelled, dropping his unusually thick French accent for the occasion.

A hand slowly set the chain in place and opened the door a crack. Canal's flashed his French secret service badge rapidly instead of his Wild West sheriff's badge, and showed his revolver holster for good measure. The mouth associated with the eye that examined them emitted a deep sigh and slid the chain off the door, admitting the two curiously attired representatives of the law.

"What the hell is going on here?" the inspector thundered, peering about in the light rendered dim by the recent breakage of several of the apartment's lamps.

The young figure who had sighed at the door, an attractive woman in her twenties with jet black hair and remarkably pale skin, remained silent and looked down at her stocking feet. The lanky young man hovering at the opposite end of the room found speech. "We were having, like, a little disagreement," he said, proving himself to be a master of litotes. "No one's been hurt," he continued.

"We'll be the judge of that," Canal retorted loudly, striding over to the girl to see what kind of shape she was in. She appeared to be neither bruised nor crying, and her clothes were intact—only the furnishings of the room seemed to have paid the price of the young couple's fury at each other, if indeed *both* had been throwing things.

Henry remained in the shadows of the doorway, his sleuth's hat tilted down over his eyes. The girl he of course knew from the clinic—he had seen Doreen's patient day after day, week after week, for at least a year—except for the past two weeks, naturally. The guy he had only seen once, but his face and build were indelibly etched in Henry's mind.

"You are Sue Spechtor, are you not?" the inspector asked the girl.

She nodded.

"Where have you been this evening?"

"That's what I've been trying to find out," her assailant cried from across the room. "I've been, like, trying to get her to tell me for the past half-hour!"

Canal looked over and examined the boy more closely. Something in his intonation was oddly familiar. Imaginatively stripping him of his Halloween disguise—the football uniform he was wearing and the black gash of antireflective make-up under his eyes—Canal suddenly recognized the shiftless musician, Doreen's former fiancé, whom he had encountered earlier

150

that week at the Stanhope Union Cemetery. "Lou Thario? What are *you* doing here?"

Lou had not yet seen through Canal's disguise, nor had he immediately recognized the alleged professor's voice without the heavy French accent. He realized who the cowboy standing in front of him was presently, but was even more confused than he had been the moment before.

It took quite some time to untangle all the threads, Canal revealing first his so-called real identity, and then presenting Henry, who finally stepped into the room, closed the door, and seated himself in an armchair not far from where the others had finally settled. Lou explained that he and Sue had been hooking up for some time—a year maybe, he proffered when pressed to provide details—unbeknown to Doreen. And Sue explained that Lou had had no idea she herself was in analysis with Doreen.

Spechtor had chosen the NIPPLES clinic because it was all of thirty yards from her apartment. Her favorite hangout was the coffee shop right across the street from her building—which just so happened to be where Lou would often kill an hour before meeting up with Doreen when she finished her clinical work. One day Sue had accidentally stepped on Lou's foot while they were standing in line to place their orders, and one thing had led to another … Doreen's place in both of their lives had only come out owing to her passing.

The inspector reflected that he had been right in supposing that Lou had accused Doreen of the very thing he himself was guilty of—sleeping around. A true *loup-garou*.

Sitting in an armchair with Canal and Henry safely between her and Lou, Sue went on. She had realized pretty early in their relationship that Lou was cheating on her, and had often complained to Doreen about the love triangle she found herself caught in. Doreen had never asked anything about the people involved, nor even if they were male or female. Sue admitted she tended to say "them" to refer to a him, a her, a man and a woman, two women, or two men indifferently—but didn't everyone these days?—and Doreen never asked for details, much less names, effectively blinding herself to the true nature of the situation.

But that did not stop the would-be analyst from dispensing advice. One week she would tell Sue to show some self-respect and break it off, the next to get even, turning the triangle into a quadrangle. Sue had been enraged at Doreen for months for constantly telling her how she should handle things, instead of letting her figure it out for herself.

Canal marveled silently that whereas Doreen had proven curious about whatever her patients said that concerned her personally, she had shown virtually no interest in things she believed had no bearing on herself. In a singular twist of fate, the most seemingly adventitious or "extimate" turned out to be most intimate, the most extraneous, quintessential ...

When questioned as to her whereabouts that evening, Sue reluctantly revealed that she had finally decided to give Doreen's unwelcome advice a try and, if not actually have a lasting fling, at least get even with Lou. The musician had been multiplying his visits to Sue since Doreen's demise, and had been accusing Sue ever more stridently of being unfaithful to him, as if he were convinced she had been unfaithful to him simply by being in therapy with Doreen. Sue had decided to give him something to bellyache about, and planned to go home with the first man who showed interest in her at a Halloween party she had heard about.

She had come up with a costume, dressed, and crashed the party, where she quickly downed a few good stiff drinks to prepare herself for something her heart was not in. "A tall, older man danced with me for a while," she explained, "and seemed to be getting really into me. I could barely stand the sight of him, and had finally steeled myself to the idea of going home with him, when he fell—"

"Fell?" Canal and Henry exclaimed simultaneously.

"Yeah, pretty unbelievable, huh? Just my luck to hook up with a total spaz. Tripped over his own feet. Seemed to come down pretty hard."

"And?" Canal asked with bated breath, his accent creeping back in.

"He sat there on the floor, rubbing his ankle, claiming he had sprained it. After that, he just sat in the corner morosely, not even bothering to try to speak to me again. Imagine this giant mummy blubbering over a little sprain when he could have had all this marvelous me," she gestured to herself from head to foot, "with no effort whatsoever," she concluded bitterly.

"At least he had at hand all the bandages he could possibly want," the cowboy said, lightening the tone. "Can anyone corroborate your story?"

"Well, if you can find a limping mummy down around St. Mark's Place …"

"St. Mark's Place?" Henry asked.

"Yeah, the party was right across the street from the bookstore."

"Did you know anyone else there who could verify your account?" queried Canal.

"No, the person who told me about the party wasn't there," she said, regretfully. "There was this witch who hit on me, though I left so quickly after she delivered her pickup line she probably wouldn't even remember me."

"That depends on what you were wearing," the Frenchman remarked, "and how long she was looking at you."

"I went as WMD," she offered glibly. "Not terribly imaginative, I'm afraid."

Canal was not sure he had heard correctly. "WD, whirling dervish?" he wondered. He asked her to repeat what she had said.

Like most of those who are asked to simply repeat something, she explained instead of reiterating. "Weapons of mass destruction," she decrypted, "you know, the George Bush fetish."

The inspector's quizzical face inspired her to jump up lithely, open the hallway closet, and extract a homemade costume from it sporting cardboard and tinfoil missiles and the giant letters W M D spray-painted across the front.

Seeing this, Canal concluded that her story bore the requisite marks of verisimilitude. But her sometime beau, Lou, jumped out of his seat and cried belligerently, "You were supposed to wear that costume with me at the party *we* were invited to, you skank! I waited for you for two hours here."

"And how many times have you stood me up or kept me waiting for ages," she riposted just as forcefully, leaping out of her armchair.

"Give it a rest, Lou," Canal stated firmly, standing in his turn and putting an end to their argument *in statu nascendi*. "You have driven the girl to almost committing a foolish act. It iz time to try something else."

Turning to Sue he added, "Getting even will get you nowhere. It is the surest path to perdition." He gestured to them both to be seated, and all three resumed their places. Reflecting for a moment, he addressed Sue anew, "The next time a therapist starts giving you advice, run the other way. Although you might initially find it relieving to be told what to do—"

"I hated Doreen's advice right from the beginning," protested the girl.

"Then why did you keep going to see her?" the inspector asked.

"I guess I just wanted to try to be like her, poised, beautiful, successful. But she got so insistent with her ..."

"Recommendations?" Henry proposed, as she seemed to be looking for the *mot juste*.

Sue looked at Henry gratefully, but rejoined, "No, they might have been recommendations in the first few weeks I saw her, but after that they were more like marching orders or homework I got graded on at the next session."

"So that's why you'd slam doors and break things on the way out?" asked Henry.

"Yeah," she admitted feebly. "Embarrassed the hell out of me, but after being given enough F's and being rebuked week after week, I couldn't help—"

"And yet you kept going back," Canal interrupted.

"At least I never kept my anger a secret—not like some of the patients I'd see coming out of sessions with her. It's the quiet ones you have to watch out for—they keep it all bottled up inside, and when they blow, look out!" she exclaimed, making a big explosion gesture with her arms. "Genuine WMD."

Canal and Henry gave each other significant glances. "Who were these silent patients with the grim faces?" the inspector asked Spechtor.

"I never learned their names—nobody talked much in the waiting room." Sue reflected for a moment and then continued, "There was this one girl, a brunette with long hair, and a guy too—he had unruly red hair. Those two came out of sessions looking like they coulda killed somebody."

"Somebody?"

"Maybe anybody."

CHAPTER TWENTY-SEVEN

It was getting on for one in the morning when Sherlock and the sheriff entered Canal's apartment building. The inspector had asked the secretary to go through the list of Doreen's patients with him to see if they could figure out which was the furious brunette with long hair, which was the steaming redhead, and who else on the list might be worth chasing down despite the late hour. Henry, who was feeling like he had been adopted by a firm but kindly uncle and swept up in an adventure that took his mind off his private sorrows, had needed no convincing.

In reply to Henry's query about Canal's magically disappearing accent, the inspector had remarked during the short car ride uptown that he too thought he had given a remarkably good impression of a New York police officer. He could imitate an American accent when he had to, he had explained, but it was rather fatiguing to him to speak that way all the time. It was unclear to Canal whether Henry had bought the story, but he had prepared it in advance—indeed, he had trotted it out on numerous prior occasions—and delivered it as if it were the most natural thing in the world.

Entering the foyer of his home, Canal noted that the silver salver on which Ferguson conveyed messages to him had been placed on the *vide-poches* immediately adjacent to the door, which was always a signal that he had an urgent note awaiting him. He reached for the tray and read the scrawled communication hurriedly. Grabbing Henry by the arm, he rushed out and hightailed it back downstairs to his car. "They're waiting for us down at the police station right now," he stated with no explanation, apparently including Henry in the otherwise royal we.

CHAPTER TWENTY-EIGHT

A haggard-looking Ponlevek greeted them at the precinct upon their arrival. The officer indicated that he had been trying to reach the Frenchman for hours. Canal first introduced Henry, whom Ponlevek had met a few weeks prior when questioning people at NIPPLES, and then recounted in brief the major events of his own evening. He did not neglect to request that Ponlevek ensure an autopsy be performed on Sorrel, testing for curare, even if the doctor who signed the death certificate indicated heart failure as the likely cause and no family members or friends requested a post-mortem. The inspector also gave Ponlevek a copy of the list of Doreen's patients, complete with their known addresses, and indicated that they might next have to question everyone around Sorrel, including *his* roster of patients.

Leading them into a room with a one-way mirror, Ponlevek explained that the bundled-up figure they saw pacing back and forth behind the mirror professed to have poisoned Doreen at the Sunday luncheon at the convention center, having slipped unnoticed into the kitchens dressed as a member of the wait staff.

"What did he give as a motive?" Canal inquired.

"Get this," cried Ponlevek, despite his fatigued state. "Says Doreen was his analyst and that he killed her to convince his fiancée he wasn't in love with her!"

"In love with his fiancée?" Canal queried, somewhat confused.

"No," Ponlevek replied as if what he had said was perfectly self-evident, "in love with his analyst."

Wanting to be sure he had gotten this straight before proceeding any further, Canal repeated, "So he claims he killed Doreen in order to prove to his fiancé that he was not smitten with Doreen?"

"Dat's what he says over and over," Ponlevek replied, shrugging his shoulders. "Never changes his story."

"Pretty extreme proof, if you ask me," Canal opined. "His fiancée must have been thoroughly convinced he was head over heels for his analyst ..."

Henry finally managed to get a good glimpse of the man's face and interjected, "It's Derek Cepe!"

"The redhead with the bottled-up anger?" asked Canal.

"No, that's Jim something or other. Derek's the one Doreen always gave extra time to—seems like his girlfriend had at least a *little* reason to believe there was something unusual going on between them."

"Hmm," Canal grunted. Turning to Ponlevek, he asked, "Does he have a convincing story about how he learned about and got ahold of the curare?"

"Says he's a toxicologist. Specializes in poisonous mushrooms and natural venoms produced by animals and insects."

"And I suppose his story checks out—you have had time to run a background check on him?"

"It's all kosher," the man in blue replied. "His official title is biologist with Hamzter, the big pharmaceutical company across the Hudson." Ponlevek picked up the report lying on the table in front of them. "He's thirty-five, was born in a small town in upstate New York, got a master's in biology at

SUNY Binghamton, moved to New York about ten years ago. No police record, no moving violations, not even a parking ticket. The only tsetse fly in the ointment is an atrocious credit report, but those are a dime a dozen."

"Among the population at large, yes," quibbled Canal, "but among scientists working for major pharmaceutical companies ... Did he give any explanation for it?"

"I didn't ask," Ponlevek replied without manifesting any sense that he had been caught slacking off. "The guy comes in, confesses to the crime, explains how he did it—how much more can you ask for?" he enquired rhetorically. "Okay, the motive sounds a bit far-fetched, but—"

"A bit?" Canal exclaimed. *"Du jamais vu, plutôt!"*

"Huh?" Ponlevek growled.

"Unheralded in the annals of criminology!" Canal glossed his French for the monoglot. "That does not mean it cannot be a real motive," he added, "but it makes one wonder."

"Yeah," Ponlevek assented, "I figured I'd let you have a crack at him before I filled out a police report with a cockamamie story like that ..."

CHAPTER TWENTY-NINE

Monday morning found Canal setting out from home in rather unusual garb, prolonging Halloween beyond All Saints' Day. Atypically dressed in an ill-fitting, inexpensive polyester blend suit, orange hairpiece slicked back, thick horn-rimmed glasses, and a beat up, bulky black rectangular briefcase in hand, he planned to present himself at the door of the apartment Derek Cepe shared with Loral Lamour, his fiancée. He would introduce himself as Mr. Lauttre, the public defender who had been assigned to Derek, as the young man obviously could not afford to retain a lawyer himself.

The weather was so positively balmy that Canal decided to alight from the cab halfway to Loral's in order to walk for a while in the bright sunlight. If this kept up, he said to himself, New York was in store for a true *été de la Saint Martin*—what did the Americans call it? The expression escaped him for a few blocks and then, when his thoughts had turned elsewhere, the words "Indian summer" popped into his mind. "Talk about different cultures," he mused.

Ambling along, he wondered at what Henry had said about Doreen's extra-long sessions with Derek. The girl may well, he speculated, have been more enamored of her patient than of

Lou, Henry, or Watkins. But then again, she may have simply loved who she felt she was when giving him advice, since— given what Derek had told Canal in the wee hours the night before—he seemed to have accepted her answers to his questions so gratefully and even complimented her on her penetrating insight.

"She appears to have been one of those analysts," the inspector said to himself, "who is constantly seeking praise from her patients as a sign of love, something that is thoroughly incompatible with conducting an analysis. She failed to realize that an analyst must love without asking to be loved in return or even wanting to be loved in return ..." Arriving at the entrance to Loral's apartment building, he appended the reflection, "And she certainly had not grasped that psychoanalysis is the fine art of responding to questions without answering them."

CHAPTER THIRTY

L oral was unreceptive from the moment Lauttre knocked at her door, never even having been informed that Derek was in jail. Canal, who had apparently interrupted her tardive breakfast, attempted to convince her to let him in, indicating that Derek himself had given him the alphanumeric code necessary to enter the building and even the key to the apartment.

The girl remained quite suspicious, however, and Canal felt she was on the verge of shutting the door in his face. "*Je travaille pour vous deux,*" he articulated distinctly in French, "*et Derek a vraiment besoin de votre aide.*"

His insistence that he was there to help and that Derek was in serious trouble, conveyed in French—even though it was not in the Acadian dialect the young man had told Canal his fiancée spoke with her family—seemed to turn the tide. Perhaps she felt that this stranger could not possibly know she spoke French if Derek had not told him. She unlatched the chain and opened the door sufficiently for Lauttre to pass through.

The contrast between Derek's clean-cut appearance and the apartment that he had been sharing with Loral for the past year could not have been starker. The walls were lined with traditional vestments and vestiges from every imaginable culture, Peruvian, Japanese, Balinese, Mexican, Chinese, Indonesian,

Mongolian, and Turkish, to name just a few of the ones Canal recognized. The muffled music that Canal had noticed in the background while standing in the hallway turned out to be Gregorian chants, and there was a faint smell of stale incense in the air, rounding out the picture of unrestrained New Age syncretism.

Books on every imaginable form of spiritual practice vied with old and new books on psychoanalysis for space on the overflowing shelves, tables, and chairs. There were even stacks of them on the floor, in no order Canal could easily divine: so many piles it was difficult to navigate the few steps into the small apartment without knocking any of them over. There was stuff absolutely everywhere!

Canal, who was no clean freak—his own study often being so covered with papers and books that his visitors found it difficult to find a place to sit—considered that the English word "stuff" was far more useful in this context than anything French could provide, the stacks of things scattered here and there not in any way being confined to books or papers, but including music disks, movies, pipes, musical instruments, beads, and even shoes. The inspector had seen some crowded apartments between Paris and New York, and had dealt with a few pack rats before, but this was a new variation on the theme to him: everything seemed to be virtually brand spanking new. No wonder Derek's credit report was a disaster area ...

Contrasting improbably with the New Age thematic, Loral's long blond hair was elegantly cut and shaped along more classically Chanel lines, just like Doreen's had been in the photos Canal had seen of her. But there was no trace of Doreen's reputed elegance in Loral's pink bathrobe or fuzzy slippers. Her distant eyes neither sought nor avoided Canal's. If she had played the role of the whirling dervish at Drago's party the other night and seen through his current disguise to perceive the Western gunslinger of Allhallows' Eve, she was playing it exceptionally cool. Her barely modulated voice, which the inspector seemed to recognize from somewhere, asked neither his name nor anything else about him—such as why he spoke French or had a thick French accent—and there was no ceremony whatsoever in the way she plopped down in her chair at the breakfast table, leaving it to Canal to decide whether to excavate for himself a place to sit on the nearby living room sofa or join her at the table.

He opted for the former and carved out a small spot for his briefcase on the coffee table in front of him. Closer inspection of the premises revealed what appeared to Canal to be two distinct strata or stages of accumulation: a stage of New Age spiritualities and cultures, and a more recent stage of things psychoanalytic and stylishly preppy. The second stage was already well advanced, given the number of pairs of expensive Italian shoes and French *haute couture* accessories.

Canal's oddly attractive hostess, whom he uncannily felt he was not laying eyes on for the first time, did not enquire as to why Derek was in jail. At the attorney's prompting, she proffered that she assumed he had been working on an experiment at the lab as he sometimes did and had spent a couple of nights on the couch in his office. His work schedule was very annoying, she told Lauttre, often getting in the way of dinner and movie plans she had made. She loved him to death, she insisted verbatim—and Canal's ears did not fail to perk up at this expression he had heard certain people unthinkingly employ, much like "to love someone to pieces," both of which spoke volumes, he felt, about what they wanted to do to those they said they loved—but it was highly insensitive of Derek, Loral went on, not to be more considerate of her!

The would-be lawyer noted that her foot did not quiver nor her hands or legs tremble when he told her that Derek was accused of killing Doreen Sheehy, Derek being the only person who knew her, he claimed, who could be suspected of having access to curare, toxicologist that he was. Loral acknowledged his profession, but asserted that there was no way he would

167

ever have committed such a crime. She seemed unflappable, ataraxic even.

When Lauttre asked her how she knew that, she simply told him, "He could not have, *un point c'est tout*." Her gaze then seemed to be attracted to the far corner of the kitchen and her lips moved as if she were reciting a mantra or prayer. "Or perhaps conversing with some unseen figure?" thought the Frenchman, who was beginning to wonder whether his uncommunicative interlocutor might not in fact be delusional.

Canal had been faced with psychotics of many ilks before, from the calm, everyday types who seemed even more like everyone else than anyone else, to the floridly hallucinating whose speech and gestures were so difficult to fathom. He realized that, if his hypothesis about Loral were correct, it was not so much that she was hiding something from him or from herself either, whether voluntarily or involuntarily, but rather that there was no pressure in her that would make the truth of Derek's activities leak out, almost regardless of what they talked about. Neurotics were dying to tell, even as they consciously endeavored to lie. But people like Loral were different, and the onus would be on Canal to divine the questions which would open the right doors.

Finding nothing better to begin with than her fiancé's atrocious credit report, the self-proclaimed public defender began, "The prosecution is going to be looking for a motive and is obviously going to latch onto your financial problems. Derek was paying Miss Sheehy at the NIPPLES clinic quite a lot of money, whereas *she* was already very well off. The girl had no surviving family members and the prosecution will undoubtedly argue that he hoped to get his hands on her fortune. How would you respond to that?"

"Ridiculous," she stated matter-of-factly. "Derek has plenty of money."

"Then why did he declare bankruptcy a couple of months ago?"

"Oh, that was just a strategy we used to get rid of some credit card debt and student loans he had hanging over his head."

"That is not what he told me," Lauttre retorted, albeit non-confrontationally. "He said you had recently received two astronomical bills, one from a lawyer and another from a therapist he had never heard you were seeing."

"I told him those bills were *bogus*," she replied somewhat exasperatedly. "The lawyers never got me anything so I don't owe them anything, and—"

"Was that the arrangement you made with them at the outset? They were only to get paid if you got a cash settlement of some kind?"

"That's the way it always works," she stated, as if it were self-evident. "That's what they all say on television."

"Did you sign a written agreement with them to that effect when you first retained their services?"

"I didn't read every word of what they made me sign. All I know is what I told them when I asked them to sue NIPPLES."

"Sue NIPPLES? Is that what the legal suit was about?"

"Yes."

"Sue them for what?"

"Wrongful non-admission," she proffered, as though it were a well-known, well-established tort.

"What do you mean by that?"

"They should have admitted me to their training program on three separate occasions and wrongfully did not," she replied with some heat.

"Did they give any reasons for not accepting you?" he queried, realizing that Loral had thus in all likelihood been the fifth applicant to the program when four out of five applicants, including Doreen, had been "unanimously approved."

"When my lawyer first contacted them, they indicated that members of the Admissions Committee were not satisfied with my answers to certain of their questions during the interviews.

169

If they hadn't asked me all those trick questions, naturally I would have done a better job," she explained angrily.

"What kind of trick questions?"

"One of them asked me in what area of psychoanalytic theory I thought I was the most lacking. If I admitted to being lacking in some area, they obviously would never have accepted me!" she concluded vociferously.

"You think not?" Lauttre asked, as quietly as he could.

"Plain as day," she responded categorically. "Another one asked me what personal quality I felt I was most deficient in that is required for being a good therapist—get real!" she exclaimed. "Each time I applied, at least one of them tried to trip me up, and so I got rejected three years running even though my analyst told me I would make a great healer."

"Your analyst told you that?" Lauttre asked, flabbergasted.

"Naturally. That's why I applied in the first place."

"You mean you applied because Miss Sheehy told you that you would make a great therapist?" Lauttre queried, even though he knew the dates did not add up. Seeing the sudden confusion in his hostess's features, and not wishing to increase her paranoia by seeming to know something Derek himself could not have told him, since Derek himself was not in the know, the inspector hurriedly added, "The police subpoenaed the list of all of Miss Sheehy's patients from the clinic—that is how I know you were seeing her."

But Canal had been confused as to the reason for Loral's confusion. "It wasn't Doreen who told me I would make a great therapist, it was the other analyst," she explained.

"What other analyst?"

"The one before Doreen," the girl replied impassively.

"The one who gave you the other astronomical bill?"

"That's the one. He strongly encouraged me to apply several years ago and said he couldn't understand why I never got accepted."

"Hmm."

"But I know why," she said, turning to look out the window past Lauttre.

"You do?"

"Sure," she said matter-of-factly. "Doreen got my spot."

"How do you figure?" asked Lauttre, who found her last remark a trifle on the nose.

"There are only so many spots per year, you see," she expounded, "and they only take so many women, so many people under thirty, and so many brunettes."

Canal's eyebrows rose to full reveille height, but the girl was looking elsewhere and did not see. Illegal as quotas might be, he could well imagine how applicants might get the impression that the Admissions Committee tried to balance the age and sex of each new entering class, but he was positively perplexed by this reference to brunettes, especially by a blond.

"Because of some stupid trick question," the girl went on, "Doreen was given my spot and has been living my life ever since. With her gone, I should finally have gotten my spot back."

"Really?" Lauttre asked, wishing to determine how far this incredible train of thought had developed, his prior speculations about Doreen having taken her own life evaporating even more now than they had while speaking with Derek.

"Yeah, they were just waiting until after Doreen's funeral to enroll me in her classes and assign me her patients— except myself, of course," she added, sniggering hoarsely for a moment. Turning somber, she added, "But then Friday I received a letter saying that I couldn't be considered for admission this year, as the Admissions Committee does not review applications from candidates who have already been rejected three times."

"You had already been rejected three times?" Canal asked the obvious, providing some speech with which to keep her talking.

"Yeah, I applied the first time the same year Doreen applied," she explained. "I remember seeing her sitting with the other

171

candidates waiting to be interviewed, just like I was. That's how I know she got my spot."

"Huh. And so this letter ...?"

"Some Institute rule, that some incompetent administrative assistant was supposed to apprize me of in a form letter as soon as I was rejected for the third time back in December, but apparently forgot to send. But there's no such rule," she declared with undisguised furor.

Canal was aware that rules at such organizations were often more honored—though not in the bard's sense—in the breach than in the observance, and waited to hear her out on the subject.

"I finally realized," she went on, "that the analyst who was supposedly helping my lawyers get me admitted—"

"You were suing for admission, not damages?" the astonished attorney asked.

"For admission," she continued heatedly, as if it were the most natural thing in the world. "The idea of suing for damages owing to malfeasance on their part was mentioned only if the suit for admission failed."

"So you were saying," Lauttre brought her back to the thought he had interrupted, "that the analyst who was helping your lawyers with the suit ...?"

"Turned out not to be helping at all," she cried, rage appearing in her eyes. "He had been secretly sabotaging my every attempt to get admitted and had even gotten the Institute to send me that letter saying I could no longer be considered for admission!"

"How did you find out?" Lauttre asked, affecting to lend credence to her story, crazy as it sounded, giving her the benefit of the doubt after having heard so many unbelievable things about the workings of psychoanalytic institutes in the course of the past few weeks.

"The bill he gave me on Friday," Loral replied as if the matter were self-explanatory.

"How do you mean?" he asked, not seeing the connection.

"He had been letting me slide on payment for ages, and suddenly gave me a bill for all those sessions on the same day I received a letter from the Institute. He obviously just wanted to drive the last nail in the coffin—"

"Coffin?" Lauttre reiterated, wondering if she intended this literally or figuratively. "He was unwilling to leave you any elbow room?"

Her pretty but not terribly expressive features now evinced confusion. "Leave me in the Elbow Room? I don't believe I've ever heard of that room. Is it a ballroom at the convention center?"

Canal noted that her mishearing was no ordinary neurotic mondegreen, for she had failed to recognize his metaphorical use of the term "elbow room." He realized that to follow up on what she had heard instead of his intended meaning of *coudées franches* would take them away from the murderous intentions she seemed to attribute to her first analyst, but he thought it worth pursuing nevertheless. "You know the convention center? The Forbes Convention Center?"

"Sure," she said unguardedly, "I work there on weekends."

"Derek told me you had been unemployed the past couple of years."

"He always exaggerates," she cried indignantly, "acting like I don't contribute anything to the household finances. I've been working part-time in food services there for the past few months."

"Do they pay pretty good money there for your services as a ...?" the inspector asked in his vulpine manner, putting the emphasis on the money even though he was really only interested in learning her position.

"The money's okay," she confirmed. "I'm only a waitress so far, so it isn't exactly the big bucks, but pretty soon they'll give me more hours and move me up to assistant manager."

Canal made a mental note to have Ponlevek check to see if she had been working at the convention center the weekend of the NIPPLES conference.

"Sounds good," he remarked, "avoiding the expression *not too shabby* that had occurred to him first, given how indirectly it said what it meant and not wishing to introduce any more potentially confusing metaphorical material. "So you were telling me that this other analyst of yours obviously just wanted to drive the last nail in the coffin—"

"Yeah, finish me off," she confirmed. "But he won't get a chance to now," she exclaimed. "I took care of that!"

"Oh," Lauttre interjected, "how did you do that? Did you go and talk the whole thing out with him?" he asked—skirting the phrase *give him a piece of your mind* he thought of first, not wishing to go down that road—even though he did not believe for a minute that this had been her approach to taking care of business.

"There was no point. It was obvious what he was trying to do to me. Just wanted my money and figured he'd never get it if I started paying tuition at the Institute. That's why he kept blocking my admission."

"Ah," the would-be lawyer exclaimed, as if seeing the light.

"I told Derek I did not owe that bastard anything, since he had never helped me in the least," she declaimed heatedly. "I went to see him so my life would get better, but he's the reason it's been getting worse! There's no way I'm going to pay for that."

"So you found a way to get him to back off and drop his claim?" Lauttre asked, trying to find some non-explosive way to discursively elicit a confession.

"I sure did," she cried, plainly proud of herself.

"How did you proceed?" he asked, affecting to be impressed by her exploit.

"I encouraged him to have a good time," she replied simply.

"And that was enough to do the trick?" Canal marveled.

CHAPTER THIRTY-ONE

L eaving Loral's later that morning, Canal moseyed over
to Seward Park to ruminate for a spell before proceeding to explore certain possible leads around the Lower
East Side. Sunning himself in the brilliant November rays, the
inspector marveled anew at the singular way in which things
so often came to light in the course of investigations. It was a
non-linear process, to say the least—a hint here, an overlooked
clue there, a hundred hypotheses formed and discarded. His
work was still far from done, yet he realized that the face of the
case had changed dramatically thanks to the interview he had
had with Derek Cepe before the one-way mirror some thirty
hours earlier.

The young man had struck Canal as nervous, anxious, and
resolute, yet not the slightest bit guilt-ridden or attempting
in some magical way to undo what he had done. He seemed
determined to be believed but showed no signs of remorse,
although he did profess to having missed talking with Doreen
the past few weeks—in *that* he seemed quite genuine.

Preferring to approach sensitive topics in a roundabout manner, frontal approaches leading so often to redoubled resistance,
the inspector had begun by asking Derek about what Ponlevek

had so poetically referred to as the "tsetse fly in the ointment": his atrocious credit report. It showed two bankruptcies, one about five years back and the other very recent. The first owed, the young man had explained, to a disastrous marriage to a woman who wanted to buy everything under the sun and refused to limit her expenditures to fit their income. The toxicologist had admitted to indulging her far more than he should have and finding it hard to rein her in.

In response to Canal's question as to how they had come to know each other, Derek had recounted that they had met at a party, had spent every minute together for the first ten days after meeting, and had married within a month. Derek had been surprised to realize, once married, that his new bride had no conception of what it meant to balance income with expenditures, and shouting matches about money had gone from once a week, to once a day, and then to once an hour in very short order. They had gone from head over heels in love to divorce within two months of their fabulously expensive honeymoon cruise in the Caribbean.

The scientist had attributed it all to being young and foolish, even though he had already been thirty at the time, and seemed to thoroughly enjoy telling the inspector about it, smiling here and there and laughing at himself. Indeed, he had waxed far more loquacious about his non-criminal activity than about his alleged crime, regarding which he provided no new details whatsoever, much less extraneous, complementary, or corroborating elements.

When Canal had enquired about the far more recent bankruptcy, Derek's mood had grown somber. He had explained that his current fiancée had been spending money like water, no matter how much he protested, and that things had come to a head a few months prior when she had received a bill for legal services amounting to half of his annual salary.

"The law firm had already sent it to a collection agency some time before for failure to pay," Derek had said.

"Legal services?"

"Yeah, can you imagine?" the toxicologist had said, shaking his hand up and down to emphasize how considerable a figure these legal expenses had come to. "We already had our usual share of credit card debt, not to mention the seventy grand in student loans I owe from college," he had added, searching Canal's face to gauge his reaction.

Affecting to share Derek's indignation at the situation by whistling at the substantial sums involved, the inspector had asked, "So bankruptcy was the only way to go?"

"The only way I could see—I had no savings, she had no savings, and there was nobody we could borrow the money from," the young man had proffered, shrugging his shoulders. "But wait till you hear the clincher."

Canal had evinced that he was all ears.

"Not only does she owe this legal firm an astronomical sum," Derek had stressed, leaning over the table to get closer to Canal, "but just yesterday I see a bill on the kitchen table, from an analyst I never even heard of, for something like two and a half years of full-fee sessions she had apparently had with him but never paid for."

"An analyst you had never heard of? How long have you been together?"

"Almost three years. I knew she had started working with a trainee at NIPPLES last year, because it was at my suggestion that she went there to deal with her virtual paralysis in life. But it turned out she had been seeing *another* guy for several years and had, for the past year, been seeing *both* of them simultaneously. We're ruined!"

"A tough situation," Canal had sympathized, wondering what could have led this young woman to consult with two therapists. Had she been playing one off against the other in the transference, he had asked himself, looking for one parent of each sex, or just trying to get as much help for herself as she could?

"I hear that Doreen was loaded," Canal had commented, as if it were a stray thought that had just occurred to him.

Derek had bristled at this. "She—I mean, I had no intention of trying to get money from her," he protested, as if to clear himself of the allegation of having been actuated by any such sordid motives.

"*She*?" Canal had reiterated.

Derek had seemed confused and tried to erase his tracks. "I just got my pronouns in the wrong order. I didn't know anything about Doreen's financial situation, until *you* told me just now."

"You could not tell she was well off from the way she dressed or the jewelry she wore?" Canal had continued in this vein even though he was beginning to get the impression that the truth of the matter lay elsewhere. Still, any topic, he had reflected, could potentially serve his purposes if pressed hard enough with someone like Derek. For—based on his slip of the tongue, his defensive reaction to its being pointed out, and his concern with being believed and approved of by his interlocutor, manifested in his constant gauging of Canal's facial expressions—the young man struck the inspector as neurotic, not psychotic.

"I don't pay attention to designers or brands or any of that," Derek had replied dismissively. "If she wore leaves and lamella, I could have told you the exact genus and subspecies, but I wouldn't know Farah Wong from Wal-Mart."

Raised eyebrows had been Canal's only response to this.

"Loral has been telling me for a while that Doreen is a very elegant dresser, has a lot of style and class, and ...," the biologist had trailed off, seemingly worried that he was revealing some kind of pecuniary motive.

"She knew Doreen?"

"Apparently saw her come in and out of the waiting room when Loral was waiting for her own analyst."

"Who was her analyst?"

178

"She never told me. Can't say as I ever asked either. In any case," Derek had added, returning to his prepared script, "Loral found Doreen so incredibly attractive, poised, and classy that she was a hundred percent convinced I must be madly in love with her and harped on it endlessly these past few months!"

"A hundred percent," Canal had reiterated with a questioning inflection in his voice.

"Like the dickens! Two hundred percent!" Derek had upped the ante, yielding to the magnetic appeal of hyperbole.

"That's a lot of percent. Do you think you ever gave her any reason to be so convinced?"

Derek had shaken his head. "None I can think of. I'm sure I told her I thought a lot of Doreen, but strictly as a therapist."

"Hmm," Canal had punctuated, hearing the "thought a lot of" as both "thought highly of" and "thought about often."

"It was because I thought so much of Doreen that I recommended that Loral find someone to work with at NIPPLES."

"Would you not find yourself lost in thoughts of Doreen now and then when you were around Loral?"

"I get lost in thought plenty, but it's usually about toxins, not women."

Canal had examined the young man closely to see if a connection between the two topics might occur to him, but none seemed to. "You do not recall ever bringing up things you talked about with Doreen when you were with Loral, or accidentally calling Loral Doreen?" he had asked, continuing in the same vein as before.

Derek had reflected a few moments and then uttered the single word, "Never."

"Has anyone ever told you you talk in your sleep?"

"I talk in my sleep?" Derek had enquired, baffled. "How would *you* know?"

Canal chuckled to himself as he recalled the unexpected flare-up of paranoia his carelessly formulated question had ignited. To douse it, Canal had explained, "I was not claiming

179

that you *do* talk in your sleep, I was just asking whether anyone had ever told you that you had been overheard talking in your sleep."

"Oh, I see," the young man had said, visibly relieved. "Not that I recall."

"So you cannot think of anything you have ever done that might have led Loral to believe you were in love with somebody else?"

"You know," he had replied in a confessional tone, "I'm not the most self-reflective guy—Lord knows Doreen told me that often enough!—but I'm really not a womanizer like some of the guys I know. I don't look at porn, I don't stare at every girl who walks by ... One is already more than enough for me."

Derek's denial had struck Canal as not so unthinkingly categorical as to fail to ring true. "So how do you think Loral ever got the idea you were crazy about Doreen?"

"She met me at the clinic one day as I was coming out of the consultation room with Doreen and that was it. She took one look at Doreen and instantly decided she was the bee's knees! I even noticed—and I'm not very observant when it comes to people, as Doreen often told me—that Loral began wearing her hair like Doreen and buying clothes and accessories like the kind Doreen had." Canal's ears had stood at full attention at this. "She would come home with outfits that looked identical to Doreen's—it was almost as if she were following Doreen around to figure out where she shopped."

Shifting positions on his park bench, Canal recalled that Derek, who had initially been thinking this sort of detail nicely corroborated his story, had instantly been hit by the thought that Loral might have been stalking Doreen. He had obviously never told anyone or even himself in so many words about Loral's changes in outward appearance over the past year. They had suddenly struck him as uncanny and his face registered horror. The words "Oh my God!" had escaped him involuntarily.

"You failed to read the writing on the wall?" Canal had asked quietly and a bit cryptically.

"I sure did," the scientist had replied, lost in thought and staring beyond his interlocutor at some unknown point on the wall. "She must have been stalking Doreen for some time. She even started talking a bit like her, although I could never figure out how she could possibly have heard Doreen do much speaking."

"*She's* the one who did it," Canal had almost whispered, "not you."

"I don't know how I could have missed all that," Derek had continued, as if oblivious to what Canal had said.

Canal had glanced at the list of Doreen's patients once more to check something. "Her last name is Lamour?" he had asked, struck by the name.

The young man had looked up at Canal suddenly. "Yes, that is Loral's last name. How did you know?" he asked. Then reflecting for a moment he had concluded, "You must have seen it on my credit report—we've got a couple of credit cards together."

"No," Canal had replied nonchalantly, "her name is on the list of Doreen's patients that I got from the clinic."

Some sort of battle had then been waged inside Derek. "Nooooo," he had finally uttered, as if trying to contradict the obvious conclusion he himself had just been forced to draw, "she can't have been in analysis with Doreen too! How could that happen?"

"Perhaps Loral requested that Doreen be her therapist, and nobody at the clinic knew of any connection between you and Loral?" Canal had proposed.

"But Doreen would have had to realize pretty quickly that she was seeing both members of a couple," he had insisted. "Isn't there some rule against that?"

"Maybe she did realize it but, given her unorthodox and rather wild analytic style, she simply didn't care," Canal had

181

proffered. "On the other hand, maybe you both referred to each other in ways that hid the truth from her."

The young man had seemed bewildered by this eventuality.

"Does Loral refer to you by your Christian name, or does she call you by some other name or nickname?"

"Actually, she calls me by my middle name, Frankie—well, it's really Francesco, but—"

"And you call her ...?"

Frankie had gotten the picture. "I usually call her Lambkins, a take-off on her last name." He had shaken his head in continuing disbelief.

"Which is obviously French," Canal had remarked tangentially.

"Yeah," Derek had replied thoughtfully. "Her family was originally Acadian and moved down from Nova Scotia to New Orleans." Seeming to get over his shock, he had added, "She even speaks some kind of French dialect with her family, although I could never understand a word of it."

"Few people can," Canal had reassured him. "So she's the one who did it, not you."

The biologist had, Canal recollected, allowed himself to hear it this time. "What gives you *that* idea?" he had asked indignantly.

"You said it yourself," Canal had replied calmly.

"When did I say any such thing?"

"When you said 'She ... had no intention of trying to get money from Doreen,' instead of saying 'I.'"

"That could give it away?" Derek had asked in disbelief.

"So there *is* something to give away!" Canal had concluded confidently.

The toxicologist had slumped down in his chair, his five exhausting hours at the police station seeming to hit him like a truck. He had appeared resigned and words had spilled out of him. "I don't know how she could have brought herself to do such a thing ... I mean, she had threatened a couple of times, but I thought it was a game. In fact," he had opined, almost oblivious to what he was saying, "I thought she'd sooner kill me than Doreen!"

Behind the one-way mirror Ponlevek had been incredulous and Henry horrified. Canal, for his part, had mused at the fatal tendency many a man had to believe *himself* to be at the center of a woman's concerns, thinking it was all about him.

"I guess I knew I wouldn't be able to keep up the charade forever," the young man had added.

"Why the charade in the first place? Are you trying to be some kind of hero for her by sacrificing yourself?"

"I know it's stupid, but Loral seems so innocent, so fragile— she'd fall apart completely if she had to go to prison."

"I would not be so sure about that if I were you," Canal had cautioned. "Some people are a lot stronger than you think."

Derek had shaken his head doubtfully and sunk still further into his chair.

Recalling his private reflection that the young man perhaps had some investment in seeing her as weaker than she really was, Canal left his place in the sun to check out a nearby costume store.

CHAPTER THIRTY-TWO

Overcoming her embarrassment at not having seen through Jean-Pierre Kappferrant's thin professorial disguise, Caroline Drago rang the bell at Inspector Canal's apartment. As was her wont, she was elegantly dressed and coiffed—indeed, she was looking particularly radiant that evening—and was more than fashionably late. She was shown by Ferguson into the main living room where the inspector and his friend Jack Lovett were having a glass of sherry and chatting about winter travel plans. They rose to greet her, Canal having no need to make introductions as Drago and Lovett had met a few years earlier.

No sooner was she seated and provided with a libation, she opened the conversation by saying, "So, my dear inspector, it seems you have been moving heaven and earth at NIPPLES! If I am to believe the last communiqué we all received from the Board of Directors, I shall soon barely be able to recognize the organization."

Lovett looked from the one to the other wide-eyed, so Canal admitted, "Yes, it is true, I have taken advantage of the leverage provided by recent happenings to force through a few changes."

"A few changes?" Carolyn exclaimed, astounded by the understatement. "Let's see, the middle group is going to be given proportionate weight on the faculty. And," she added pointedly, "from now on the Admissions Committee will be composed of six members selected annually by lottery from the *entire* institute faculty—meaning there will almost certainly be offsetting votes against any candidate being promoted by one group strictly for political reasons."

Lovett objected, "How did that happen?"

"That's just the beginning," Drago protested excitedly. "Henceforth, all students will be required to take a new course designed to help clinicians recognize and treat psychosis, from its most ordinary forms to its most flamboyant. And," she looked from the one man to the other expressively, "at the outset, all faculty will be required to attend this course too! No more supervisors like Watkins, Doreen's overseer, who hadn't a clue that Loral Lamour was a paranoiac. From now on, they'll be able to detect psychotic patients who may have slipped through the screening process estab—"

"Screening process?" Lovett almost fell out of his armchair. "What screening process?"

"Oh," she replied volubly with a flippant gesture of her hand, "did I forget to mention that? How silly of me. Winnicott's advice to teach students to treat neurotics first, before introducing them to work with psychotics, is finally going to be implemented—at least to some degree, since the screening committee will inevitably make mistakes."

Lovett was incredulous. He looked to Drago to see if she was serious, and she reiterated that this was what was indicated in the memorandum she had received not two days before.

She confessed that she could hardly believe it herself. "It seems that our trainees will no longer need to spend ten years getting rid of the education in their art that it took six or eight years to acquire," she concluded, paraphrasing Ezra Pound's reflection.

"I tried to get them to eliminate the distinction between training analyst and ordinary analyst as well," Canal said modestly, "but they absolutely refused to budge on that point. I guess Americans are still not yet ready for it, unlike most of the French and South Americans who gave that absurdity up ages ago. Whereas one's most crucial training as an analyst comes from one's own experience undergoing analysis, the training analyst system tends to turn personal analysis into a farce, forcing candidates, as it often does, to work with people they are not comfortable with and do not respect or trust. But a little horse trading had to be done," Canal added philosophically, "and they were willing to change almost anything other than their precious hierarchy."

"Where in heaven's name did all of this leverage come from?" Lovett asked, eyeing Canal keenly.

"I threatened to sue them for criminal negligence," Canal explained, sipping his sherry. "I realized, after talking with you a few weeks ago about the American Psychoanalytic Establishment's refusal to do anything about the blatant abuses at NIPPLES, that there was no point going through the usual channels. They would have made a show of carrying out a thorough investigation and then swept everything under the rug."

Drago and Lovett nodded in vigorous agreement.

"APE would no doubt have established a new Committee on Committees at NIPPLES, piling one more dysfunctional layer onto the others," quipped Canal. "It is the same in business and government too. People prefer to concoct something new to append to the existing structures rather than fix the foundations."

"So I went with my friend Ponlevek from the NYPD before the Board of Directors and argued that any district attorney in his right mind would agree that it was tantamount to criminal neglect to allow a young student like Doreen to work with patients like Loral. Doreen was woefully unprepared to work with paranoiacs, and she was being supervised by Watkins, a man incapable of even recognizing one."

The inspector paused here to take another sip of his drink, and then, seeing that his audience was watching him expectantly, continued, "Naturally, the Board threatened to sue me for gathering information without a warrant. But Ponlevek made it clear I was working closely with the NYPD on the matter and then I threatened them with a second count of criminal negligence."

"What was that?" asked Drago, intrigued.

"Failure to ensure that Doreen met the criteria for admission, which she clearly had not. She had never completed her Psy.D. and had even been dismissed from her program for ethical violations. Not that I think a Psy.D., or for that matter an M.D. like Sorrel's, amounts to a hill of beans in helping one practice psychoanalysis—*au contraire!*"

"Nor I," Drago quipped, "but still, I guess you rather had them by the throat there."

"Yes," Lovett agreed, "I guess you did." He drained his glass and placed it on the coffee table in front of him. "You never did tell me who killed the young analyst-in-training—who was this Loral Lamour you mentioned?"

Before Canal could reply, Ferguson entered the living room and announced that Thanksgiving dinner was served. The party of three rose to their feet, and Drago and Canal proceeded to the candlelit dining room, where a roaring fire was blazing in the hearth, while Lovett disappeared for a few moments into the powder room.

Taking the seat the inspector held out for her to his right at the beautifully set table, Drago, the luster of whose hair was seen to fine advantage in this lighting, commented, "Your friend Lovett is quite a handsome fellow—I barely had a chance to notice when I met him during the site visit, but he looks like a rather delectable morsel."

Canal laughed at her description, noting the voracious overtones, and spoke as follows, "Jack, if I may be allowed a word of caution, does not go for the frontal approach, preferring to be the pursuer, not the pursued. If I am not sorely mistaken," he added, looking Drago in the eye, "he enjoys the subtleties of the game of seduction at least as much as the grand finale, if you catch my drift."

Her brow furrowed for a moment, but soon smoothed. "Have you, by any chance, been talking with Jocelyn?" she asked, playfully reproaching Canal for listening to gossip with a shame-on-you hand gesture.

"I have, not that there was any need to, though. Your own actions spoke more loudly than any of Jocelyn's words."

"Well," she said resignedly, "I guess I *can* be brutally direct, and end up scaring many a good man away." She gave Canal a meaningful look, allowing him to conclude that he himself might well be counted by her as among the many.

"Jack's a keeper, not some fly by night Johnny. And, to the best of my knowledge," he added, shooting her a significant glance, "you will not be poaching him from anyone, so there is no need to pounce. Why not try to let him come to you?"

Lovett could now be heard approaching the dining room, so Drago gave the inspector a conspiratorial wink.

CHAPTER THIRTY-THREE

As the velvety butternut squash soup laced with a few thin slices of chorizo was served, accompanied by a delectable red Corbières "La Pompadour" of 2000 vintage, Lovett reiterated his question about who this mysterious Loral was, whom he had never heard of before. They clinked glasses and tasted the potage while Canal stated his conclusion that she was someone for whom Doreen Sheehy was the ideal woman, everything she wanted to be and become.

As Lovett looked just as perplexed as before, Canal backtracked and explained that, after years pursuing every kind of New Age spiritual path, Loral had stumbled upon psychoanalysis via Jung's concept of synchronicity. She had eventually applied to the NIPPLES training program at the same time as Doreen. Loral later became convinced that she had not been granted admission because Doreen had gotten her spot—not only in the program but in general—and that Doreen would have to be eliminated if Loral were to reclaim her rightful role on the stage of life.

Her delusion had gone so far that she believed that from the moment of Doreen's disappearance, she would be granted Doreen's place in the program, moving directly into the fourth year, and resuming work with all of Doreen's patients. She even expected to take up automatically with Doreen's boyfriend, Lou, who she apparently saw for the first time at the convention center the night before she pricked her with a poison-tipped needle.

"The boyfriend too," Drago exclaimed. She raised her wine glass toward the inspector and gazed at it with a look of sheer delight attesting to the lusciousness of its fast diminishing contents.

"Oh, but her delusion went much further still," Canal commented, after nodding gratefully in recognition of her compliment and refilling her glass. "If only I had been able to find the fateful words uttered by her analyst that let the genie out of the bottle, making Loral *se goubliner*, turn into a delusional beast, I could have had her *dé-lire* them, read them backwards."

His guests looked at each other in total bewilderment.

"What are you talking about, man?" asked Lovett.

"In the old days, in Normandy, it was believed that you could reverse the effects of a magic formula by reading it backwards, making it as if you had never read it in the first place."

Lovett, relishing both the delicious wine and the curious connection between *lire*, reading, and *délire*, delusion, but literally un-reading, asked, "You think Doreen herself triggered Loral's break?"

Canal nodded vigorously. "I think there's a very good chance of that. I suspect Loral had managed to live her life quietly seeking guidance from one spiritual tradition after another, and had begun reading psychoanalysis the same way she read Buddhism and Sufism. It was probably not until Doreen began making 'deep interpretations' of everything she said to her that her delusions began and she became a menace to herself and others."

"Many a clinician inadvertently triggers a psychotic break. But I suspect it isn't easy to isolate the exact phrase or sentence that did it," Lovett opined regretfully, as he polished off the scrumptious soup, "even if one could return the evil genie to the bottle by having the subject recite it backwards."

Drago, who was bored with such word games and hypotheticals, sipped her wine appreciatively and remarked, "It's a shame it so often requires a dramatic incident of this kind for transformation to occur in organizations. People hold tenaciously to their positions, as if they were holding on for dear life, until a crime—"

"—or a lawsuit," Lovett interjected, transparently referring to the giant lawsuit the Alliance of United Psychotherapists had successfully brought against APE a couple of decades before.

"—or the threat of a lawsuit owing to a crime," Canal interjected in turn.

"—forces them to change ever so little," Drago concluded.

"Perhaps you two and Edgar, our other analyst friend from the Scentury Club, could start a new association of non-aligned analysts—NANA, you could call yourselves," Canal remarked half-jokingly.

Drago's eyes glittered, the idea of working so closely with Lovett seeming to resonate nicely with her burgeoning feelings toward him. Still, her decades working in organizations left her less than enthusiastic about such a group's prospects. "I'm sure it would be very pleasant at the outset," she said, smiling at Lovett, "but then little by little we would become like the three rabbis with four different opinions: Edgar would become the champion of the untraditionally non-aligned, Lovett here—"

"Call me Jack," Lovett interjected affably.

"Jack," she amended, happy that her new love interest had made the first gesture, "would spearhead the non-traditionally unaligned, and I would be left heading those who wished to remain traditionally non-aligned."

"That's only three factions, not four," Lovett upbraided her teasingly.

"I believe our host's wines are a little too potent for me to come up with a fourth," she replied, laughing. "I've gone adrift in all the privatives."

As Jack seemed similarly disinclined to find a fourth in their hypothetical group, Canal, who was happy in the private reflection that his guests *avaient le vin gai*, opined, "Yes, I suppose that the formation of such blocs is inevitable ..."

"But not necessarily disastrous," Lovett opined. "It is only when factions are artificially forced to remain together by the likes of APE that internecine warfare becomes inevitable. Otherwise each division could go its own way as soon as its supporters were numerous enough."

"Hmm," Canal pondered this for a few moments. "Pluralism is the new fascism," he opined.

"Especially enforced pluralism," Lovett commented, nodding spirited assent. "It makes everyone bitter, and breeds hypocrisy and back-stabbing."

"Let us not forget gossip," Drago interjected. "It's part of the fallout of repressive tolerance."

"No, indeed, let us not forget it," Lovett exclaimed. "When, instead, splinter groups are allowed to go their separate ways, they often experience a period of flourishing innovation. They feel freer, no longer desperately defining their positions strictly negatively with respect to those of another faction."

"Yes, a flurry of creative activity sometimes ensues as a new phoenix rises from the ashes of the old school," Drago agreed. "Still, were it not for the attractions of working with a few select colleagues, it almost makes you want to abandon all ties to institutions altogether."

"Yes, I can well imagine," mused Canal, who had jettisoned his ties to assorted sordid associations over the years and had once been heard to say that he knew what it was like to "cohabit with household waste." He added, "I get the impression, though, that most analysts feel incredibly insecure about their right to practice if they do not have a giant organization backing them up, attesting to their having the proper credentials. The less they feel they were transformed by their own analysis and the less convinced they are that they are helping other people change, the more they crave a guarantee—some sort of Good Housekeeping seal of approval from an international licensing body."

"Indeed," Lovett concurred, taking a thoughtful sip of water. "Rather than letting their results speak for themselves, finding confirmation of their theory in clinical successes, they keep looking for some outside agency—some great repository of knowledge and legitimacy, some Other—to assure them they are doing the right thing. As if the people running that authorizing body could have any greater claim to guaranteed knowledge of theory and practice than they do!"

"Ah," Drago interjected ironically, "but there is such safety and comfort in numbers. Not content to be certified by the analytic institute one trained at in one's own city, one prefers to be certified by the regional association, then the national association, and then by the international association—the bigger the better!"

"Pretty soon," Lovett upped the ante, "everyone will rush to become part of the Interplanetary Psychoanalytic Establishment, and then the Intergalactic Psychoanalytic Establishment, in the hope that the bigger the establishment, the more omniscient it will be and the more reassuring the investiture it will provide."

"What will they do, then," Canal asked, baiting his companions still further, "when the Nalackians across the planetary pond form a rival Transgalactic Psychoanalytic Association that has even more members?"

"The bigger the authority, the more cover it provides," Drago declaimed, laughing. "Since they are less concerned with quality training than with getting the nod from the bureaucratic powers that be, practitioners will be forced to join the new association."

"So there will be a sort of run on APE's intergalactic bank?" Canal joked.

"Maybe," Lovett conceded, "though more likely both intergalactic entities will publish false membership figures in the attempt to stem defections."

The three friends laughed for some moments at the absurdity of the imagined scenario, which was nevertheless all too likely—as they each well knew—to come true someday, if indeed it had not already.

"The urge to appeal to experts and authorities seems irresistible," Canal remarked, scanning the mirth. "You expect that from the populace, but not from analysts."

"An expert is nothing more than a nincompoop from the next town over," Drago quipped, "as one of my neighbors used to say."

"And yet everyone seems to want their approval. Businesspeople consider their legitimation to come from the market, which is their expert," Canal mused aloud. "They believe their decisions to develop certain products are validated if they manage to sell more than other manufacturers, even if their products turn out to be dangerous, whether socially or environmentally."

He gave his soup a contemplative taste and then added, "Students believe that their colleges have the requisite knowledge to authorize them to do whatever it is they are training to do, when schools are often simply bastions of the current orthodoxy."

"Trainees at a place like NIPPLES at first think the faculty possesses the knowledge requisite to transmit the mantle of legitimacy to the next generation," Drago opined. "But once they begin to realize their teachers are mostly a bunch of knuckleheads and kooks, they begin to look elsewhere for the seat of knowledge and ratification."

Lovett chuckled at the lovely woman's apposite choice of words to describe her colleagues, and relished the connection between seat and *derrière*.

"The students are never made to realize," Canal concluded, pursuing his own train of thought, "that *no body* has any sort of absolute, guaranteed knowledge. They go through their entire training without ever encountering the foundational fact that there is no guarantee, whether in theoretical physics or in any other field. Every theory is just a theory, and as such incomplete and open to revision. Every science to date has undergone paradigm shifts that limit or overthrow the validity of everything that had been considered to be true before."

"Which doesn't stop analysts from striving to convince their trainees that the institute's faculty, or the international body, actually does have some arcane, mystical absolute knowledge," Lovett interjected. "They pretend that *their* group has managed to corner the market on truth."

"It's their way of ensuring transference to the institute—getting the students to worship and identify with the school—and of ensuring a continual flow of new trainees and money," Drago quipped.

"Right," Canal murmured, drawing the word out indefinitely, beginning to see the motive for the absurdity. "Even though it thwarts the all-important liquidation of the transference at the end of one's personal analysis, *ça fait avancer le schmilblick!*"

Seeing Drago's uncomprehending features, Lovett glossed the inspector's argot, "It keeps things moving along, keeps bringing in new suckers." She smiled in appreciation for the explanation.

"Some transference to the institution is inevitable at the outset," Lovett observed, "and even helps put the students to work. But rather than systematically call into question the students' naïve belief in a complete, all-explanatory theory, the faculty act as if they possess one, insinuating to the students that they are too inexperienced or dense to grasp it."

"I guess the faculty will do just about anything to make a buck," Canal commented, smiling wryly. "Perhaps such organizations are, in a sense, fated to ossify and, worse still, become self-defeating after a while," he postulated pessimistically, "and the only solution is to periodically dissolve them or secede from them. After all," he added platitudinously, "bureaucracy is bureaucracy, even when its posts are occupied by 'enlightened' beings, who have supposedly been thoroughly psychoanalyzed."

CHAPTER THIRTY-FOUR

Ferguson, who had been hovering near the door for some moments now, waiting for a propitious pause, punctuated the conversation by entering the dining room, clearing away the soup, and serving the main course.

Drago, who was always more interested in people and their passions than in institutional matters even at her own school, admired the plates the valet set before them and said to Canal, "You told us Loral's delusion went much further than simply believing Doreen had taken her place—who else was involved in it? Anyone *I* know?"

"Well, you remember the analyst dressed as a general who dropped dead at your Halloween party?" Canal asked.

"Sam Sorrel? Don't remind me," Carolyn cried. "For God's sake, tell Jack my party was wonderful! Didn't I do things up right?" she asked flirtingly.

Canal assured Lovett that it was a marvelous party, and that the general, a member of NIPPLES by the name of Sorrel, had met his maker through no fault of Caroline's. "It turned out he had been serving as Loral's analyst for some three years."

Drago and Lovett expressed due astonishment that Loral had been seeing two shrinks simultaneously, both affiliated with the same school, and Canal went on, "Sorrel had encouraged her to apply to the Institute's training program, apparently thinking she would make a fine therapist, and had helped her lawyer sue NIPPLES for wrongful non-admission and malfeasance."

"He helped her sue his own institute?" exclaimed Lovett, incredulous.

"There are more things in heaven and earth, Horatio …," Canal quipped.

Drago nodded. "Truth is often far stranger than fiction."

"He was obviously duped as to her ability to work with patients," Canal continued. "And he engaged in various con-traindicated practices, like not asking her to pay her bill for years. Perhaps he was enamored of her—she was, after all, a rather good-looking lass—or hoped to receive some payment in kind from her. Maybe he even wanted to use her to settle accounts with people he disliked on the Institute's Board … In any case, I suspect he himself was pretty far gone—at least that would explain why he found Loral perfectly normal and as fit to practice as he was."

"You appear to be telling us about *his* delusions, but you promised to tell us about hers," Drago said mischievously, placing in her mouth a morsel of the moist turkey prepared *à la* Georges Perrier. "I admit he sounds mad as a March hare, but still a promise is a promise."

Canal laughed somberly at this, and commented, "Yes, he certainly had delusions enough to resell, I mean to go around. You would hope analytic institutes would do a better job keeping the worst nutcases out of the fold, but they just go on graduating Bions, Masud Kahns, and the like. Psychotics *can* contribute interesting ideas to the field now and again, and maybe a select few can practice effectively, but the human toll is often appalling.

"In any case," the inspector went on, after taking a bite of the tender turkey, and reflecting that it took a Frenchman like Perrier to figure out how to cook a good old American Thanksgiving turkey, "for reasons that will likely remain forever unknown to us, Loral was presented with a bill for hundreds of back sessions on the very same day she received a letter from NIPPLES telling her that her fourth application for admission could not be considered. She had been rejected on three prior occasions—"

"Wow!" Lovett interrupted. "She must be the only applicant to have ever been rejected by NIPPLES since its founding." He dipped his fork into the tart but sweet cranberry sauce which had obviously been made from scratch, not poured from a can.

"Must be, given that they have a ninety-nine percent acceptance rate," Canal concurred. "Anyway, three rejections was the official limit according to the statutes. All applicants were supposed to be informed of that immediately after their third rejection, and they apologized for the administrative slip-up, but that was the way it was."

"She must've immediately assumed there was a connection between the bill and the letter, since she received both the same day." As Canal nodded, Lovett continued his speculations, "She figured that Sorrel was being two-faced, pretending to help her gain admission, all the while conspiring to block her admission—she probably even thought that he was the one who sent the letter, or at least ensured it was sent."

"Precisely," Canal agreed, awed by his friend's guesswork. "She was suddenly forced to consider the possibility that he had never actually believed she had what it took to be an analyst, which was a direct blow to her idealized image of herself. It must have been mind-bogglingly impossible to her to fathom how someone could be as perfidious as she believed he had been, and lead her on for so long. She just *had* to find some kind of explanation for it."

He paused for a moment to taste the side dish of sweet potato pie. "The twofold explanation that came to Loral in a flash and that became cemented as an unshakeable certainty was that he *did* believe she would make an excellent analyst, but—one, he did not want her spending money on tuition, wanting her money for himself, and two, he was convinced she would be such a good analyst that she would steal all his patients away from him!" As his interlocutors smiled at this, the inspector remarked, "It is quite an ingenious and elegant solution, when you think about it, even if it relies strictly on the principle *is fecit cui profuit*. It worked very well to patch up what threatened to become a serious rent in the fabric of her universe."

Drago, whose jaw had been dropping lower and lower for the past few minutes, almost knocked her wineglass over as it slipped from her hand. She protested, "You're scaring me! Dr. Wilkins said Sorrel died of heart failure, but you're making it sound like murder."

"Well, I, for one," Canal replied calmly, "never believed he died of heart failure, regardless of what the good doctor wrote on the death certificate. I figured that whoever had killed Doreen had struck again."

"You mean Loral was responsible for ruining my party?"

"I had not yet even heard of Loral at that point, as I had no clue who killed Doreen," Canal replied. "But I was struck by the whirling dervish who was dancing with Sorrel at your party shortly before he collapsed. It seemed to me that the young woman in that costume had arrived at your penthouse just minutes before and was gone just moments after his death, as if she were some sort of angel of death. No one I asked had any idea who she was."

"So who was she?" Drago enquired, dying of curiosity, and secretly wanting to strangle whoever it was.

"I never found out. I tried—"

Canal's sentence was interrupted by Ferguson, who burst into the room saying, "I'm sorry to interrupt, sir, but there's a call from Inspector Ponlevek—he says it's urgent!"

The three givers of thanks looked at each other blankly and Canal involuntarily uttered, *"Mon Dieu*, could there have been yet another murder?" He jumped up and followed Ferguson into the foyer.

CHAPTER THIRTY-FIVE

"What was so urgent that it couldn't wait?" Lovett inquired as Canal returned to the dining room.

The inspector appeared to be slightly shaken. "Somebody was assaulted, but I could not find out *who* because the phone line went dead suddenly. I could not reach Ponlevek at any of the numbers I have for him," he added frustratedly, "so I shall simply have to wait for him to call back. Cell phones render me crazy!"

As their host lapsed into a preoccupied silence, Drago asked him, "Did the officer say anything else?"

"Huh?" Canal muttered, coming out of his trance. "Well, unless my ears are playing tricks on me, the person who did the assaulting was Wilma Watkins."

"What?" cried Drago. "Wilma?"

"Who is she?" asked Lovett.

Drago explained that Wilma was a specialist on Amazonian tribes at City University who had been married to the analyst William Watkins for thirty years, but was recently divorced. "I don't believe Wilma could have seriously attacked anyone," she concluded.

"Maybe I was mistaken," Canal declared. "Let us give it no further thought until Ponlevek calls back."

Ferguson appeared with a small tray containing three shot glasses, which he distributed to them, before busying himself removing the dinner plates, bringing in the desserts, and stirring up the fire so that it was blazing brightly again.

Lovett held up his glass and looked quizzically toward Canal. The inspector explained that, given the size of the Thanksgiving meal, he thought it well to include a pause that, in Normandy at least, was reputed to clear the stomach and make room for what was to follow—in this case, three different pies: pumpkin, apple, and pecan. When asked what the foreign brew was that performed such miracles, he replied that it was Calvados, and that the tradition was that it was to be drunk *cul sec*, that is, all at once, after pronouncing the magic formula: "*Trou normand.*"

By this point in the meal, Canal's guests were willing guinea pigs to any culinary experiments he wished to conduct, so, shouting altogether *trou normand*, they downed their applejack and felt it begin to burn its way through the prior course.

"We must be careful not to *dé-lire* the formula," Lovett exclaimed, "for were we to pronounce it backwards, its marvelous effects might immediately be reversed."

"And then we would have no room for these delectable looking pies," Drago agreed, "which it would be a true pity to let go to waste."

She raised to her mouth a bite of the pumpkin pie she had selected among the three desserts Ferguson had just offered, and reminded the inspector that he had been telling them about the whirling dervish who had spoiled her fun on Allhallows' Eve.

"Oh yes," he nodded. "Based on Inspector Ponlevek's conjecture, I had been looking for someone at the Institute who might have served Wilma Watkins as an accomplice in taking revenge on her ex-husband for leaving her in order to run off with Doreen. But half the faculty and half the trainees wanted Doreen dead, and most of them knew the former Mrs. Watkins, which got me nowhere. Jocelyn Josephs, the librarian, helped put me on the right track by mentioning Doreen's many disgruntled patients, and it struck me that the young whirling dervish might well have been one of them."

Canal now recounted in a few words how he and Henry had first followed up a false lead, but that the loopy confession made by Derek Cepe, Loral's fiancé, had put them on the right scent. He next described at some length his interview, masquerading as Derek's public defender, with Loral, and commented, "It was when I asked her how she had managed to get back at the second analyst she was seeing—I did not yet know it was Sorrel, but I suspected as much since she seemed of about the same stature as the girl in the whirling dervish costume—that things got a bit dicey."

"How do you mean?" asked Drago.

"Well, she told me she had simply encouraged Sorrel 'to have a good time.' When I remarked that it must have been some good time and asked what its effect had been, she bridled and asked what this had to do with Derek and Doreen."

His interlocutors indicated they could see her point, and Canal, after taking a small bite of pecan pie and chewing for a few moments, continued, "I feigned nonchalance, saying that I was curious because the prosecution would be likely to think that analyst's astronomical bill was pretty important, potentially making Derek desperate enough about his financial situation to do something rash. If she had found a way to get the debt cancelled or forgiven, it might help his case.

"But she was not buying it," he added. "I had the impression I saw a gleam of pure murderous rage in her eyes, and then her manner changed abruptly. Her body relaxed and her legs shifted into what in another woman might have been a sensuous posture. She cooed about having told silly ol' Derek she had taken care of the bill and that there was no cause for worry. Then she began playing the gracious hostess and offered me tea—to keep me there long enough to prick me with curare, I suspected."

207

"How did you handle that?" Drago enquired admiringly, something Lovett did not fail to notice and take fleeting umbrage at.

"I professed lack of thirst, but she insisted I try her delicious English breakfast. As English as the Black Prince and Jack the Ripper, no doubt," Canal exclaimed. "My apologies, Jack," he bowed to his guest. "I figured that if I tried to stay and continue the discussion, but thwarted any attempt she made to approach me, she might slip some other kind of poison into the tea, or resort to less refined methods of manslaughter. So I simply made a show of looking at my watch and jumped up, exclaiming, 'O my God, look at the time—I have an appointment uptown in ten minutes!' I thrust a calling card in her hand, apologized for not being able to stay for tea, told her I would be in touch regarding the accusation against Derek, and dashed out the door."

"A narrow escape, perhaps," Drago opined, smiling at the inspector, and noting that he did not apologize for not having done something more apparently heroic.

"Yes, perhaps," Canal confessed. "I was quite convinced by then that she was mentally deranged, and even marveled at the common theme in the so-called trick questions Loral had been asked by the NIPPLES Admissions Committee during her interviews—in what aspect of psychoanalytic theory she thought she was the most lacking and in what personal quality required for being a good therapist she felt she was most deficient. I thought them exceedingly useful for detecting possible psychosis in the course of an ordinary academic or job interview, since they asked her to say something about her own lack or possible inadequacy in knowledge or character. Someone like Loral has a great deal of trouble locating lack of any kind that is related to herself, the world being full when one has rejected repression, instead of being riddled with holes, lacks, and losses, as it is for us neurotics."

"Yes, they are astute questions," Lovett agreed, "surprisingly so given the lamebrains who asked them. But you still didn't know, after interviewing her, how she got even with Sorrel."

"Indeed, I did not," Canal admitted, "and the problem was that I was convinced she had killed Sorrel in the exact same way she had killed Doreen. I don't know why—I guess I was not very imaginative, or simply wished that since I had finally solved one crime, the other was somehow miraculously solved in advance. What I failed to realize was that the two murders were thoroughly asymmetrical."

"Asymmetrical?" asked Lovett. "How do you mean?"

"Doreen was a woman with whom Loral had confused herself," Canal explained. "To attack Doreen was thus to attack herself, or at least her externalized ideal of herself, and she had no intention of destroying her own beauty, which she felt to be crucial to her success in the world. That is why she opted for a poison that paralyzes the body but leaves it perfectly intact."

"Whereas Sorrel was a man," Drago interjected, "and an authority figure who suddenly shifted from being a supposedly helpful other to being a persecutor who was doing everything imaginable to thwart her from achieving her main aim in life."

"Exactly," Canal said, approving his new friend's firm grasp of things.

"Though why anyone in her right mind would want to be an analyst is beyond me," she giggled. "Unless it was to meet a man at one of the myriad conventions," she added, smiling coquettishly at her fellow shrink.

Leaving his guests to their volley of glances, Canal resumed, "At any rate, virtually everything about the two victims was different: Doreen and Loral were alike in age and sex, and both had studied some psychology. But Sorrel was twice Loral's age, of the opposite sex, and had trained in medicine. Loral could not have cared less whether he was disfigured or even dismembered in death and proceeded quite differently with him."

Lovett and Drago's features evinced that they were once again listening to the inspector's tale.

"I wasted several hours checking every costume store in a one-mile radius of Loral's apartment for red whirling dervish outfits, convinced she had come to the party, entranced Sorrel, and poisoned him. I even searched her apartment when she went out to see if I could find any portion of the costume so as to confirm my suspicion.

"All to no avail." Swallowing another bit of pie, he went on, "It finally dawned on me, looking at the pictures of herself she had in her apartment, that she was the young woman I had collided with coming out of the coffee room at NIPPLES my first day there who was so anxious to measure her new office for drapes. She must have dyed her hair blond soon after that as she readied herself to take over Doreen's role, and was even mistaken by Henry for Doreen on Halloween morning. I should have paid more attention to the fact that this young woman never reappeared at the clinic in the whole course of the investigation. She went missing and I failed to follow the missing link."

Not having been privy to Canal's dream the night before the Halloween party, his audience could not gauge the relevance or depth of the inspector's self-reproach. To his credit, he reminded himself, the only picture of Doreen he had seen prior to his run-in with Loral at the clinic had been of her body slumped over on a convention luncheon table, her face hidden by tousled blond hair. He would have been hard-pressed his first day at NIPPLES to notice the resemblance between the two young women, especially since Loral was still a brunette at that point, yet it bothered him nonetheless. "Four out of five applicants" had been unanimously approved by the Admissions Committee, and there was an unaccounted-for trainee at the clinic, if only for a day. For one who prided himself on his attentiveness to lack and to the supplement or One Too Many, it was a considerable oversight, whose consequences were all too evident ...

"So what about Sorrel?" Lovett prompted his friend, for he had lapsed into silence, and was dawdling over the unctuous pumpkin pie in front of him.

"The coroner's report came back negative for curare," Canal expounded meditatively, "but positive for clonazepam, a benzodiazepine often marketed as Klonopin."

"So curare wasn't the cure for all that ailed her?" Lovett quipped, as he relished the homemade deep-dish apple pie on his own plate.

Drago laughed genially at the handsome diner's pun.

"It was not even clear she had anything to do with it—based on the morgue's findings, it might not have been murder at all," Canal remarked. "Several of—"

Ferguson appeared at the dining room door and announced another urgent phone call from Inspector Ponlevek. Canal hastily excused himself and went into the foyer.

Drago and Lovett exchanged glances full of concern, but shortly these gave way to gazes of another tenor ...

CHAPTER THIRTY-SIX

When Canal returned, it was not clear from his countenance whether there was something to worry about or not.

"There was no fire?" Drago queried.

"Wilma Watkins really did assault someone," Canal replied.

"Seriously?" asked Drago, incredulous.

"Well, I'll let you be the judge of that," the inspector answered playfully. "She threw a lamp at the chairman of her department. It probably would not have hit him, since she aimed to one side, but he ducked the wrong way and it hit him square in the face—broke his nose, he claims."

"Assault and battery with a lit weapon?" Lovett joked.

"I guess so," Canal conceded. "And she said things were *less* asinine in academia than in analytic institutes!"

"Maybe she'd take that back now," Lovett said, laughing, and the others joined in his laughter. "I, for one," he added, the *trou normand* seeming to have loosened his tongue still further, "think *all* organizations—whether governments, businesses, schools, or what have you—function just as badly as psychoanalytic institutes. Anyone who believes the contrary is just kidding himself! Everything goes to pot," he continued, warming to the subject, "as soon as there are more than two people involved in anything—"

"And are there not always?" Canal interjected. "Was it not Freud who said that even when two partners are making love, there are already six people involved?"

They all burst out laughing again, putting a stop to Lovett's nascent tirade, but not to Canal's private reflection that even when they adopted the trappings of democratic process, virtually all organizations degenerated into the tyranny of whoever yells the loudest, protests the longest, or curries the most favor.

"I guess Jocelyn was right again," the inspector remarked aloud. "She thought Wilma would sooner kill her ex-husband than any mistress he might have." Sipping some sparkling water, he added, "It turns out her chairman's name is William Tompkins, and he goes by 'Willy,' just like Wilma's ex-husband did. I guess if Wilma was going to lash out at someone, it had to be a Willy." Contradictory lyrics of an old song flashed through his mind, "... wouldn't have a Willy or a Sam," and he tried to recall from whence they came.

As their host fell silent once more, Lovett prompted him anew. "You were telling us that based on the coroner's report, Sorrel might not have been murdered after all."

"Right," said Canal. "Although clonazepam is taken by plenty of people for anxiety, it is not typically taken by psychoanalysts, so I felt it worth looking into. Several of Sorrel's patients told me that he kept a bottle of pills on his office desk, and more than one of them had been informed by the man himself that he had a serious liver condition.

"Yes," the inspector avouched, seeing the smirks on his interlocutors' faces, "like so many misguided souls, he seems to have enjoyed talking about himself with his analysands. Was it the typically psychotic failure to acknowledge rules or just the silly self-disclosure encouraged by certain contemporary schools of therapy? It can be hard to tell these days, but in Sorrel's case I suspect it was the former.

"In any event," he went on, "Loral must have been pretty savvy about medications, for she replaced his liver tablets in the jar on his desk with the benzos when she went to her last session with him Saturday afternoon—her fingerprints were all over the bottle. It was just a few short hours before Caroline's party, which she knew about, like everyone else who had anything to do with NIPPLES. Klonopin is strenuously contraindicated for liver conditions and combines exponentially with alcohol."

"Which explains why she encouraged him to have a good time at the party," Lovett concluded cynically. "Kind of creepy, when you think about it." He accepted a slice of apple pie from Ferguson, who was now proposing second choices from among the desserts.

"Any idea where she got the Klonopin from?" Drago enquired, as she accepted a small slice too.

"It's not very hard to get nowadays, whether on the street or by prescription. But my best guess," Canal opined, "is that she swiped them from Doreen."

"Doreen?" Drago queried, stunned.

"Yes, Doreen's boyfriend Lou told me that Doreen was totally hooked on what he called pain pills, and I suspect she must have often left them out on the desk in her consulting room at the NIPPLES clinic. She was, it seems to me," the inspector remarked, "well on her way to becoming a new Ruth Mack Brunswick, the famous analyst who was a morphine addict and shopped by phone and talked with rental agents about vacation homes while her analysands were on the couch!"

Canal's dinner guests both laughed heartily at this, having heard the story, and being aware of similar if not worse behavior on the part of their own contemporaries.

"Henry," Canal resumed once the hilarity had subsided a bit, "the secretary at NIPPLES, told me he often saw Doreen

215

playing with her purse, taking a plastic prescription bottle out of it and putting it back in again, and frantically dashing to the bottled water station, pills in hand."

"Then she deserved the name Doreen, so similar in sound to Dora," Drago interjected. "As I recall, Dora spent a session with Freud opening and closing a new purse she had brought with her that day."

"So there is someone," Canal exclaimed overjoyed, "at NIPPLES who knows her Freud! I will ensure that you are the one assigned to teach the yearlong course on Freud's original texts that I convinced the Board of Directors to begin requiring starting next fall—assuming you are willing, of course," he said, winking at her.

Drago indicated that such a course was news to her, but added, with a slight blush and a wink back, that she would like nothing better than to offer it.

Canal was pleased that his newfound friend was so accommodating. And given how chummy she and Jack seemed to be getting, he speculated that he could probably talk the latter into visiting NIPPLES once a week to teach the course on psychosis. Maybe he could even convince the pair to take on Derek and Sue as low-fee patients. "Perhaps I can even prevail upon Lou Thario to go into analysis," he said to himself, getting carried away with his future projects, "and twist Edgar's arm into taking on a musician who plays only the occasional charity event."

Seeing Drago pick up her purse and withdraw a handkerchief, Dora again drifted into the inspector's mind and he mused aloud, "It seems fitting somehow that Doreen was confused by Loral with herself, when Doreen, if she had not genuinely confused herself with Dora, was at least masquerading as her."

"As Rimbaud says, 'I really is an other,'" Lovett remarked.

"You expect us to believe that you have been indulging in the reading of poetry lately?" Canal said, ribbing his friend.

"I thought you never read anything other than serious tomes on serious subjects by deadly serious authors."

"Actually," Lovett replied good-naturedly, "I believe I came across Rimbaud's line in a book by a Parisian psychoanalyst you yourself recommended I read some time ago. I forget his name now …"

"You see," the inspector said as if in an aside to Drago, "Jack really is all work and no play. I've been trying to reform him, but to no avail. I suppose it would require someone with far greater charms than my own to distract him."

The End